At this hour Kit was so accustomed to the complete silence of the big house that when he first heard the sound, he paid no attention to it. A moment later, he distinctly heard a rustle and a soft sigh, and he was then conscious of a chilly prickling sensation at the nape of his neck. The old story of the forlorn bride of Troy Court again flashed into his mind. With an effort he went to the door and threw it wide open. He then had a clear view of the wide parquet stairs which led to the first floor.

Down them glided a figure in white.

**HEIRESS APPARENT**
by **Laura Conway**

# HEIRESS APPARENT
## BY LAURA CONWAY

A NATIONAL GENERAL COMPANY

HEIRESS APPARENT

*A Bantam Book / published by arrangement with
The McCall Publishing Company*

*PRINTING HISTORY*

*Originally published in England 1966
McCall edition published August 1970
2nd printing ... September 1970
3rd printing ... November 1970
Bantam edition published February 1972*

# Heiress Apparent

# CHAPTER 1

In the confusion of packing, the small room, usually almost as bare and neat as a nun's cell, was overflowing. Garments hung over the back of the one chair; shoes, boots, and slippers littered the floor; sponge, soap, toothbrushes and nail brushes, jostled other toilet articles, and a small traveling clock on the chest of drawers. A plaid traveling bag with a chain by which to carry it lay on the bed; the trunk with dangling straps stood with its lid thrown back and occupied much of the floor space. It was already almost full. Arabel had thrown her belongings within, regardless of its limited capacity. She was leaving Seacrest College forever, and anything that was left behind could be sent after her.

Her heart was divided. At one moment she could have whirled around in a wild abandon of joy, and at the next she could have wept for that which had brought about her longed-for freedom. Once, twice, there had been a knock on the door, and a youthful voice had asked pleadingly to be allowed to help. Surely there was something . . .

"Not a thing," Arabel had said firmly, and on the second supplication, "I shall do better by myself, Charlotte, and you, surely, should be occupied with your French preparation."

At this the door softly opened. A face showing traces of tears appeared round the edge of it. "Not today.

Have you forgotten? It's the half-holiday for Miss Norton's birthday, and prefects were given permission to go into Richmond for tea and do shopping if they wanted to. You were to have taken us."

The voice was woebegone. Arabel sighed, but was constrained to pay some attention. "I'm sorry, Charlotte, to have disappointed you, but it was unavoidable and all such a rush. I must catch the three o'clock train."

"Couldn't you have waited just one more day—until tomorrow?"

"Impossible. There will be a great deal for me to do when I get home. My mother must be distracted. She needs my help."

"If only I could come with you."

"Do not be absurd, my dear."

"But it isn't so absurd—not really. It is nearly the end of the term and my home is in the same county. My parents won't mind if I miss the last weeks. They know what a deep devotion I have for you. And as I am to spend the summer holidays with my uncle and aunt in Trouville, I shall see nothing of you for ages."

"You have been looking forward to this holiday, Charlotte."

"Yes—because I thought that when I returned in September you would be here as usual; but now . . ." Tears spilled over.

Arabel said, "If you can manage to step across all the things on the floor, you can sit on the bed while I finish packing. I had hoped to be able to spare you ten minutes before I left, but there may not be time."

Charlotte uttered a gasp of gratitude. She picked her way carefully through the debris but ended by taking a flying leap which landed her in the center of the narrow bed. She huddled there, wide serge skirt tucked around her.

"Miss Norton told you, I suppose," said Arabel.

"Oh, yes, and the others too. She sent for us and explained why we could not go out this afternoon.

There was no other mistress available, she said. As though I should have wanted to go with anyone else. It wasn't as though I had anything important to do—only to get away for a few hours and to be with you. Oh, Arabel, please tell me, why should Lady Thora's death mean that you leave here forever? She wasn't a relation, was she?"

"Certainly not, but I have known her all my life, and she has been very good to me. My mother was, as I told you, only her housekeeper."

"Then why . . . ?"

Arabel was scarcely less puzzled than the girl who questioned her, but her mother, in the letters which had been received that morning, one addressed to herself and the other to the principal of Seacrest College, had been emphatic. Arabel must return to Troy Court at once and she would not be coming back. Lady Thora had died nearly a week ago, and Arabel could not imagine why she had not been informed of it until after the funeral, nor why her mother should now be pressingly in need of her. The future loomed so mysteriously uncertain that she wisely endeavored not to think of it.

"My dear child, it would take far too long to explain," she said.

"Don't you care, not the least bit in the world that we are to be parted—perhaps forever?"

At this Arabel did experience a twinge of regret. Charlotte Frewin adored her and her adoration had been encouraged. She was the most wealthy and important boarder at Seacrest College and had done more than she realized to make Arabel's position there agreeable. The lot of a pupil teacher was not usually enviable. Too often the girls had little respect for one who had recently been on terms of equality with them, and the accredited mistresses expected subservience. But Charlotte, sixteen and a prefect, had made it plain to the entire school that anyone who gave Arabel trouble would have to reckon with her. Even Miss Norton, aware of the girl's devotion, had treated it with respect. Charlotte was clever as well as rich. She was one of the few parlor boarders and was given special privileges. Among her fellow pupils she had prestige. When her parents visited her, they asked especially to meet Arabel Gibson and had thanked her for her kindness to their daughter. Charlotte had been at another school where she had been so unhappy that she had been allowed to leave. At Seacrest she had stayed for two years and had settled down. She was an only child and much indulged. Sir James and Lady Frewin had worried about her, wishing her to mingle with other girls, but they had almost despaired until this affection had sprung up between her and the young pupil teacher who had herself been educated at Seacrest College. Lady Frewin had approved of her. Arabel had struck her as being in every way desirable. Though not precisely beautiful, she was neither plain nor gauche. She had charm and dignity. Charlotte had become so much more manageable since knowing her.

Secretly, Arabel acknowledged that she did have a special fondness for this spoiled child and that when she was less confused she would be bound to miss her. Although Arabel did not know her mother's plans, she anticipated that she would have to find another similar position, and if so, influential people such as the Frewins would be useful. It was really extraordinary that she was being removed from a situation in which she was giving satisfaction. Miss Norton had said that after two years as a pupil teacher she would be promoted to a junior mistress. As she was tired of Seacrest College and had no love of teaching, this was by no means an ideal destiny, but at least it meant security.

"Of course I care," she said gently, "but, as you say, we live within a reasonable distance of each other and shall probably meet."

"But are you sure you will be living at Troy Court?"

Arabel was by no means sure. The most likely thing

was that her mother with the rest of the staff would be paid off now that Lady Thora was dead. There were no near relations, only distant cousins who lived in Ireland. Would they be Lady Thora's heirs?

"I have been told nothing as yet," Arabel said. "You mustn't be too upset over this parting. Even without me you will be happy here."

"Never! I shall ask Father and Mother if I can leave."

"That would be a great mistake. Miss Norton would be upset."

"But I wouldn't have stayed longer than the first term but for you. I detest all these stuffy schools with their endless rules, and the girls are so silly, with not an idea in their heads beyond coming out, having a season, getting married, hoping it will be to someone rich and handsome."

"That's perfectly natural, Charlotte."

"It's shockingly dull. If you are not coming back, why shouldn't you be my governess? I'm sure I could persuade my parents."

"Could you? I expect they would require someone much older. There are only three years between us."

"You don't *look* older than nineteen, but you act older. Mother might think it a solution. I've never been forced to do anything I hated. I suppose that's because I'm the only one. They wanted a large family, but it didn't happen. It's the same with you. You are an only child."

"Not exactly. Ursula married twice and has twice been a widow. I have a half-brother. He's six years older."

"You never told me that."

"My dear child, there are a great many things I haven't told you."

"Are there?" Charlotte was hurt. "You said once I was your friend, not only a pupil, and we have talked about lots of things. About your mother, and how Lady Thora paid for your education here."

"I dare say that is generally known." An inverted snobbery occasionally induced Arabel to refer with cold pride to her mother's humble position and her employer's generosity. Always she had been conscious of the gulf between herself and the rich girls who had expensive clothes and an extravagant amount of pocket money. From the first it had been understood that if considered satisfactory she would one day teach there. Many times her mother had told her she must make the most of her opportunities. Better, far better, for her to teach in an exclusive school than to undertake domestic drudgery. There were few positions available for girls of refinement. The puzzle of why she was to be so summarily removed nagged at Arabel.

Charlotte persisted, "If my people agreed, would you consider it?"

Arabel, who had now thrust the last of her belongings into the trunk and hoped there would be sufficient room in the plaid traveling bag for numerous small articles, slammed down the arched lid. "Come sit on this while I buckle the straps," she said.

Charlotte clambered down from the bed. She was a tall girl, with a thick, fair plait of hair and round, pink and white cheeks. She was pretty enough now and when she had fined down she would be lovely in a fresh, English way, reflected Arabel, inclined to regret that she, with her dark hair, magnolia cream skin, and slanting green eyes, looked anything but typically English.

Charlotte knelt on the trunk, which Arabel then strapped.

She stood up, and Charlotte, with an impulsive movement, caught at her hand. "We could have such wonderful times," she said. "I'd be a credit to you, I promise. History is the one subject I really enjoy, and although you've not been allowed to teach anything advanced here, it's the thing you care about, and you've put in a lot of study, haven't you?"

"Yes, but for my own pleasure," Arabel replied.

"That's selfish. Knowledge ought to be shared—I want to share it." Charlotte was half-laughing, but she was pleading too. "There's so much I want to know. I could persuade Mother that people of my age often leave school and have private coaching."

Arabel shook her head doubtingly, but she was flattered. "My dear, I wish it could be," she said kindly.

"Then if you do, really and truly, promise me that if Mother agrees, if she suggests a trial, you won't refuse."

"I suppose it's safe to promise as much as that." Charlotte, she thought, was offering her a refuge should she need a refuge. She might. There was no telling. If only she really understood her mother. "What I do in the future depends to a great extent on Ursula," she said.

Charlotte ventured to express a curiosity she had hitherto repressed. "It's odd, the way you always call your mother by her given name."

"It's just a habit, brought about because Lady Thora always addressed her as Ursula. I picked it up as a child, and they both thought it rather amusing. I dare say I should have dropped it if I had seen more of my mother—though she has never been particularly motherly. I've always felt she was closer to Lady Thora than to me. Anyway, Ursula is an attractive name, don't you think?"

"Not as attractive as Arabel, nor as unusual. I've never heard Arabel before."

"It was the name of Mrs. Browning's elder sister. She was very friendly with Lady Thora's parents, and I suppose Lady Thora suggested it when I was born. I was born after my father's death. It must have been terrible for Ursula. She had little joy in me, probably."

"I wish you had been born into my family—my own, dear sister."

Life, thought Arabel dryly, would certainly have been very different for her had that been the case.

Charlotte clung closer to her and they kissed. Then Arabel glanced at the small clock yet to be packed. "I really must send you away," she said. "In ten minutes the cab will be here."

Although the June evenings were long, it was dark before the end of the train journey. Arabel hoped the station cab would be available and was astonished when she was accosted by a footman from Troy Court. A carriage had never before been sent to meet her when she returned, infrequently, for holidays. One was here waiting for her now, however, and without comment she followed the man from the station. She did not know him. He must have been engaged during the last year. It was over a year since she had seen the house she called home (though it had never been exactly that).

It occurred to her that it might have seemed much more her home but for her mother, who, though nominally the housekeeper, had had much influence. It was Ursula Gibson who would not allow Arabel to forget that she was the child of a paid employee and had been given houseroom at Troy Court solely through kindness. Dimly Arabel could remember the days when she had been too young to understand this and had been blissfully happy. There had been the dame's school to which she had gone each day. She had learned how to read and write, and how to do the rudimentary arithmetic in common with the children of tenant farmers and small shopkeepers. She had liked this well enough, but the real joy had lain in her freedom to roam the grounds of Troy Court. She had climbed trees and been given rides on the horses by good-natured grooms who had held her firmly in the saddle. There had been a swing and a hammock in the orchard and she had paddled in a shallow, ornamental pond where a fountain played. Her mother had been too fully occupied to give her a great deal of attention, and Lady Thora was an invalid. Rheumatism, Ursula had said, and there was nothing to cure it. On her good days, Lady Thora could walk slowly, leaning on a stick or on Ursula's arm, but she was often in bed or in a wheelchair.

It had been a sad existence, Arabel supposed, though alleviated by wealth and every possible comfort. With it all, Lady Thora had been cheerful and uncomplaining—kind also, and generous. There had been no obligation to send Arabel to the expensive Seacrest College, to provide her with adequate pocket money and clothes. Sometimes she suspected that her benefactress would have been even more generous but for Mrs. Gibson's restraining influence. She could respect her mother for this. No mother could have denied a daughter such willingly proffered advantages, but her pride would not permit her to accept extravagant indulgence.

These last few years there had been much talk of curative spa treatments for rheumatism, and for once Lady Thora had been obstinate and had insisted on staying at various hydros and clinics for weeks at a time. Although there had been a trained nurse to accompany her, she had also insisted on Mrs. Gibson's company. They were such old friends she could not do without her, said Lady Thora. The underhousekeeper was well trained and could look after Troy Court. This had meant that Arabel spent the holidays at Seacrest College, which had resulted in no holidays at all, for there were always a few pupils who lived in far-distant foreign lands and had been sent to England to be educated because hot climates were unhealthy for the young. As a pupil teacher, Arabel was expected to look after them. Once Lady Thora had written regretting that Arabel was unable to join them at Cannes for Christmas, but Miss Norton had pleaded that she was indispensable and Mrs. Gibson had written at the same time, stressing that it would ill become either of them to trespass further on Lady Thora's generosity.

Arabel had felt that it was Ursula who did not want her, rather than that Miss Norton did want her—a suspicion not without bitterness, though she had long schooled herself to resignation.

But now she undoubtedly was wanted. In the letter received that morning it was as though Ursula Gibson grudged each hour that kept them apart.

Although Arabel gazed out of the carriage windows, it was too dark to distinguish familiar landmarks. The carriage was luxuriously upholstered, with many soft cushions, for in it Lady Thora had taken all her airings, and Arabel knew that even when she was conveyed abroad, this particular carriage and her favorite horses had gone with her. Her heart was sore when she thought of the dead woman who had been so good to her. She had not been given the least chance to repay her and very little chance to express her gratitude. There had been formal letters, of course, and needlework presents for birthdays and at Christmas, but if Arabel had been allowed she would have helped her mother to look after the invalid. It had sometimes occurred to her that she could be a more diverting companion than Ursula. For one thing she was musical, which her mother was not, and Lady Thora had loved music.

These random reflections were dismissed as the horses turned in at the lodge gates. The avenue was long, but, as they came to the end of it, Arabel saw to her astonishment that light flooded the sweep of the gravel immediately before the great house. The doors were flung wide open as though to welcome an important personage. On former occasions the station fly had deposited her at the side entrance and her mother had not always been there to welcome her. This evening, tall, handsome, and composed in her black silk dress, Mrs. Gibson stood just within the hall, and when Arabel descended from the carriage and entered, her mother put her arms round her and drew her close.

"My dear child, home at last!" she said.

Arabel drew back from the embrace to stare at her. Such a greeting sounded theatrical to her, and the fact that Ursula's voice was a contralto intensified this effect. Arabel was gently urged through the hall toward the open door of the library, a large room with massive furniture and book-lined walls, which as a child she had thought gloomy. Lady Thora's father, the late Earl, had been something of a scholar and had added many rare books to the existing collection, but Lady Thora herself had cared for nothing beyond the lightest novels and had rarely set foot in the room, though fires had been periodically lighted in the huge grate and the valuable boks had been meticulously tended.

Evidently it had of late been in use, for there were signs of feminine occupation—Ursula's worktable and on the desk a bowl of flowers.

Although it was June it was unseasonably chilly, and the log fire which leapt in the grate was welcome. Comfortable chairs were drawn up to it and between these there was a table spread with a white cloth and laid for two with glass and cutlery. Arabel noticed that some of the best family silver was displayed. While Lady Thora was alive it had been reserved for her use.

"You must be starving," said Ursula Gibson, "and since it is past the dinner hour, I thought a cold meal would be more convenient. There is hot soup, of course. Nobody cares to eat alone, so I waited to have my supper with you. Sit down, dear child, take off your hat and cloak and I will put them in the hall. They can be taken upstairs with your luggage."

"I'm travel dusty." Arabel was peeling off her gloves.

"Oh, then, perhaps . . ."

"But I am even more hungry than dusty."

"Eat first then, child, and later if you wish you can have a hot bath. I have had the Chinese room prepared for you."

Arabel's astonishment was now unconcealed. The Chinese room was one of the grandest at Troy Court.

Lord Melbourne when Prime Minister had slept there while visiting Lady Thora's parents. "But—but why?" Arabel asked.

"It is only fitting. Later on you may prefer Lady Thora's suite, but I imagine you would scarcely care to take possession of it as yet. She died there, poor love. To me it is a cause for real thanksgiving that we were at home—though only just in time. A fortnight ago we were in Italy and had thought to remain there for the summer. The warm climate suited her. She couldn't have enough warmth and nobody was more surprised than myself when, without warning, she said she wished to return to England, that she had a great longing for her own home which she had not seen for months. It must have been a presentiment, for within a few days of our return she was taken seriously ill, and in less than a week she was gone."

Arabel said nothing immediately. She *was* hungry, and the cold viands looked delicious. There was a cold chicken, also a salad, a selection of homemade cheeses, and a bowl of fruit. Soup was being kept hot in a silver tureen above a spirit lamp. Mrs. Gibson indicated where Arabel should sit, and when the soup was put before her she started to eat. It was not until her plate was empty that she said in a dazed voice, "Isn't this rather unusual? Other times when I have been here we have always had meals in your sitting room."

"But that was over a year ago. Margaret Harris now has that room. It is her own domain. I told her that when you arrived nobody was to intrude upon us, as we should have much to discuss. The supper was to be left here and we could wait upon ourselves."

"Why yes, of course." Arabel remembered that in former days a young maid in process of training had waited upon the housekeeper, but apparently her mother had been promoted to a different position. That was not really so surprising, as the underhousekeeper had been in full charge during Ursula's long sojourns abroad.

Lady Thora had not, Arabel supposed, wished to dispossess the woman when they returned.

"Are we to stay on here?" Arabel asked.

The question was answered by another. "You always had a great affection for Troy Court, had you not?"

"Yes . . . but . . ."

"My dear child, as I told Margaret Harris, we have much to discuss, but you will find it less exhausting when you have eaten."

Although this was perfectly true, Arabel was gripped by a not unaccustomed spasm of irritation. Her mother's calm, inscrutable manner was nothing short of maddening.

Between mouthfuls of chicken and salad Arabel observed her, surprised to find so little change in her. Grief and dismay she must have felt at her employer's death, but it had left no trace upon her features. Ursula Gibson was a good-looking woman, but many people had said that her pleasant expression was even more striking than her fine eyes and regular features. In this there was something that suggested great kindness and a concern for one and all, a pervading warmth. There was a twinkle of humor also, a quality of which Ursula was not devoid. She could be an amusing, stimulating companion. This Arabel knew, though she had had little of her mother's company. It did not occur to her that the impression Ursula conveyed was false, only that she had never had the benefit of it. Even in her earliest childhood her mother had been sparing of caresses—of reproofs also.

Arabel had once heard her say to a woman friend, perhaps in answer to criticism, "I am not a demonstrative person." At the time she had not understood the word, but it had stayed in her memory and she had wondered. Had she been older she could have refuted it, for Ursula, on the infrequent occasions when her son visited Troy Court, was certainly demonstrative. The boy lived with a brother and sister-in-law of Ursula's first husband, an arrangement which dated, Arabel had been given to understand, from her mother's second brief marriage. A visit to his father's relations had become permanency. Did she secretly resent it because her daughter but not her son had been left to her care?

But there had been a demonstrative display of affection this evening. Ursula had welcomed her as never before.

Without appetite now, Arabel forced herself to finish the slices of chicken on her plate, but shook her head to cheese or fruit. "Cannot we talk now?" she asked.

Her mother assented, "Yes, when this has all been cleared away."

The bell rope was pulled. A young maid, with as little noise and as much speed as possible, removed the dishes. Ursula Gibson drew up her chair to the fire, and Arabel sat opposite to her.

# CHAPTER 2

"If this document had come to light earlier you would naturally have been sent for, but, as I have just told you, it was discovered only by accident. I did think there must be a will of later date than twenty years ago, for Lady Thora sometimes hinted at it, but Mr. Brecknell, the lawyer, knew nothing of it. Then, on the evening before the funeral, I was in her boudoir and casually noticed that one of the drawers of the escritoire was not properly closed. Something had slipped down behind it, and I found this sealed envelope addressed to Mr. Brecknell. I had one of the footmen take it immediately to his home, and yesterday it was revealed that this was indeed Lady Thora's last will and testament, drawn up by a solicitor in London two years ago. We stayed there for a week at a hotel, if you remember. You came up by train for the day and had luncheon with us there."

"Yes, I remember," said Arabel.

Lady Thora had been especially kind to her; in her gentle, unemphatic way she had obviously been pleased to see her. There had been emotion in her gaze as it had rested on Arabel, and to Mrs. Gibson she had said, "There is such a likeness . . ." Swiftly, the other had agreed, "To her father? Yes, there is. She is the image of that portrait I showed you."

Although there was no particular significance in this interchange, it had lingered in Arabel's memory. More important to her than had been the souvenir gifts brought from Austria. Her mother's present had been a large silk handkerchief to wear in lieu of a fichu. It had been hand-painted with pictures of Austrian girls and young men dancing in their national costumes. Arabel had never worn this gaudy trophy. It was still folded neatly in the sachet that had accompanied it. But Lady Thora had given her a charming filigree necklet and brooch and bracelet that Arabel *had* worn at school parties when her usual dark alpaca dress was discarded for one of light-colored silk.

"Lady Thora was much improved, she could move with comparative ease after the Vienna treatments," Mrs. Gibson continued. "One day there was necessary shopping for me to do. She had written a list. The nurse was on holiday, and I left her resting on her bed at the hotel. I realize now that she seized the opportunity while I was absent to visit this solicitor. Undoubtedly she had had correspondence with him, giving her instructions, for the document must have been drawn up ready for her to sign. The hotel porter, I presume, called a cab for her, since I had the carriage—and she drove to this office in Cheapside, where she signed the will and it was duly witnessed. Mr. Brecknell says it is perfectly in order."

After a pause, Arabel, who was feeling half-stunned, asked dazedly, "Do you know the provisions of the earlier will?"

"I do. There was a bequest to me of five hundred pounds, and all who were in Lady Thora's service at the time of her death were to be given a year's wages. The house, the entire estate, was to be sold, and the resulting funds with all else that Lady Thora possessed —a considerable capital—were to go to selected charities, most of them obscure and of small importance. This will had been drawn up by Mr. Brecknell's father soon after the death of Lord Riba. It was a strange will, but at that time Lady Thora was in a strange state of mind, steeped in grief. Her father had always been charitably minded, and I suppose she got it into her head that he would be best pleased if his fortune eventually benefited what she described as lost causes. They were that indeed, for today many no longer exist. The bequest to me was generous, for I had been in her service only a short while, had recently made a second marriage, and might have left her at any time. Your father was in the Navy—he was the quartermaster of his ship, and we were often separated for months. You came—but I have told you about this before."

"I know I was born after his death."

"He contracted a mortal fever and was buried at sea. Before then he had been at Devonport for a few weeks, and I had stayed with him there. His death was a terrible shock to me, especially since, at about the same time, I realized I was to have his child. I was very ill, and Lady Thora was goodness itself to me. It was feared I might fall into a decline, and she insisted on taking me to Switzerland, where you were born months later."

"But this will had been made before then?"

"Certainly. Why do you ask?"

Arabel pressed trembling hands to her forehead. "I'm so confused. I want to get everything straight in my mind."

"You are not likely to do that within an hour, my dear."

"No. Did Lady Thora make any mention of her cousins in Ireland in either will?"

"She did not. Why should she? They were completely out of touch with her and had been on bad terms with Lord Riba."

"Was provision made for the servants in this new will?"

"The bequests to them are exactly the same, except that Margaret Harris receives a legacy of two hundred pounds. No doubt Lady Thora wished to reward her for the capable way in which she has filled my position. My bequest has been increased to three thousand. As for the rest—I have told you . . ."

"But I can scarcely believe it, and I don't understand. Why *should* Lady Thora have left me Troy Court and the bulk of her money? She was always good to me. I was very fond of her and grateful to her, but could she possibly have been not in her right mind?"

"If so, none of us, least of all Dr. Galbraith here, and the doctors who looked after her when she was away from home, suspected it."

"But she was attached to you, not to me. It would have been more natural had she left everything to you, who looked after her, since she was no longer interested in these charities."

Ursula Gibson shrugged and said without any particular expression, "Well, she did not, and I have no complaint. She has treated me generously and no doubt she surmised that whatever your future, you will be equally generous to me. In some ways she was a strange woman, and she was accustomed to have her own way. I may as well be candid and admit that she never wanted you to leave Troy Court. She would have preferred it had you lived here, helped me to look after her, played the piano to her, accompanied her when she drove out, and so forth."

"I would have been glad and willing to do that and more," said Arabel.

"But I was not willing, my dear. I was ambitious for you. You had too good a brain to be wasted. It never occurred to me that Lady Thora would make you her heiress. How could I consent to such a meaningless, lapdog type of existence for you? Very little future in it. Lady Thora's heart was affected after that severe attack of rheumatic fever she had when you were a baby, and it's surprising that she lived as long as she did. After a few years of waiting on her you might have found yourself penniless and with no situation and only a village school education. I pointed this out to her, and finally she agreed that you should be sent to a good boarding school, and she became interested in your progress. All your school reports were sent to her, which was her right since she was paying the fees. She knew you loved Troy Court and would look after it."

"But so do you love it—surely."

Ursula's smile was enigmatical. "You are not likely to turn me out. My dear child, on the whole it is more fitting that you should inherit. I have never been more than an upper servant, with no education except such as I picked up through my association with her. You, thanks to her, poor love, have been reared as a lady, and, when the first shock has passed, you will adapt yourself to this position. There is plenty of time. Lady Thora arranged for a trust fund, Mr. Brecknell tells me, and, until you are twenty-one, the management of your affairs is in his hands."

"Does that mean I shall have no real power for over a year?"

"I am sure Mr. Brecknell will be loath to coerce you in any way." Ursula, with an affectionate smile, put her hand over Arabel's that were clenched in her lap. Arabel looked down on that hand as though she had never seen it before. It was many years since her mother had been required to do menial work, yet it was the hand of a worker—large, strong, with slightly thickened fingers and square nails neatly trimmed. Ursula came of humble stock. Her father had been a tenant farmer in so small a way that he was scarcely more than a laborer, but she had been a good-looking girl, and both her marriages had been to men in a better social position than herself. Her first husband had been an architect.

"I don't know why I said that," Arabel murmured apologetically. "It's not that I want power, and I should be feeling happier now, only that I'm conscious of the unfairness to you."

"But I have told you that I am entirely content."

"Yes, and you are being quite noble about it. You devoted yourself to her, and . . ."

"Do you expect me to be jealous of my own daughter?" inquired Mrs. Gibson with a smile at once tender and amused.

Gazing at that calm, benevolent face, Arabel was incapable of saying what was in her mind. She had misjudged her mother, but Ursula must never know it. From the age of twelve her life had been lived largely at Seacrest College, and Ursula had expressed no more than a perfunctory regret, even when Arabel was left there for vacations; but now with so much of her mother's love made plain to her, she realized that the sense of deprivation had not been solely on one side.

"We need never be parted again," she said.

"Never is a long time. You will marry, Arabel, though you must be sure you are loved for yourself alone and that you know your own mind."

"I don't think I am particularly impressionable. I may never marry. Ursula, tell me about Kit. How is he? Have you seen him lately? Did Lady Thora remember him in her list of bequests?"

"She did not. Why should she? She scarcely knew him."

"No—but she knew how you had grieved to be parted from him and how dear he was to you."

Far dearer than herself. Even her present knowledge of her mother's ambition for her and her steadfast determination that she should not become that soul-destroying appendage, "a lady's companion," could not alter the fact that Christopher, the son of her first marriage to John Herald, was the light of her eyes. On his few brief visits to Troy Court years ago, Ursula had been transformed. She had yearned to spend every hour with him and must have grudged the time given up to her domestic duties and the companionship of which Lady Thora could not be deprived. Arabel did not wonder at this, for her half-brother was clever and handsome and had an engaging personality. It was cruel that Ursula had felt herself obliged to give him up to the Herald family. Here again, maternal unselfishness had allowed her no choice. The Heralds were well-to-do, they could give Kit advantages that were beyond his mother's means, and the situation had been the more painful for her because the Heralds had strongly disapproved of John's marriage to a girl socially beneath him. When, after his early death, they had offered to make themselves responsible for his son, it had been on the distinct understanding that Ursula would not visit him or make any claim upon the family.

"It is over five years since I have seen Kit," Arabel said. "In your letters you seldom mentioned him. But you did say he now had his law degree. That was some months ago."

"Yes. Kit is now working in his uncle's firm. He and his aunt are very well satisfied with him, I believe. It has long been my wish to buy him a partnership."

"*Buy* him one! But Kit has been almost an adopted son to the Heralds."

"Nevertheless, partnerships are usually a matter of barter. Also, the Heralds, though they may be attached to Kit, are not impulsively generous." Ursula made these observations dryly, and Arabel wondered how much of her own salary had contributed to Kit's education and his support as a child. The Herald's despised her, but had probably not objected to accepting money from her.

"I can help you now," Arabel said, "so why shouldn't I buy a partnership for Kit? Or better still, why should he not set up for himself as a solicitor?"

Ursula shook her head. "Dear child, you must not anticipate. You can do nothing of that kind before you are of age, and before then . . . well, Kit may have his own plans. I should not be surprised, though I can say nothing with certainty. He is a good son. He writes to me regularly, and, in spite of all objections from his uncle and aunt, he has seen me as often as possible, but I am not fully in his confidence."

How could she be, thought Arabel, when she had been deprived of her maternal rights? "How hard everything has been for you," she said, "and hard for me too in a lesser degree, for I hardly realize I have a brother. Now I'm full of curiosity. Has Kit fallen in love perhaps? Is he thinking of marriage?"

Natural though this would be, a pang pierced Arabel's heart, and she was not surprised by the clouding of her mother's face. An early marriage would probably set Kit further apart from them.

"If so, I have heard nothing of it," Ursula said.

In the Chinese room all was peace and luxury. Arabel was at last alone there and she had no inclination to sleep. She had had a warm bath. A maid had unpacked her trunk. Mrs. Gibson, having seen that she had all she needed, had left her.

The Chinese room was so called because of the heavy embossed silk panels that lined the walls. Many years ago this silk had been brought from China by one of Lady Thora's ancestors. It must then have been almost unbearably vivid, but now the bright colors were somewhat dimmed. Even so the panorama of gardens, pagodas, mandarins, and charming Chinese ladies in gorgeous raiment, basking beneath trees, or leaning on pedestals beside pools where fountains played and lotus flowers floated, was brilliant. The furniture was elegant and toned in with the decor; chairs were upholstered in dull gold, the pale carpet was velvet soft. Adjoining was one of the four bathrooms which Lady Thora had had installed when deciding on certain modernizations. It was the most luxurious suite at Troy Court, and the fact that it had been alloted to Arabel was the symbol of her altered status. None the less she would have preferred one of the more ordinary guest rooms. It was true that she would have been miserable in the suite overlooking the park where Lady Thora had recently died.

The memory of her would be too haunting, but the Chinese room was said to be actually haunted by the lovely Manchu bride of the Earl of Riba of Georgian days, whom he had met and married on the customary grand tour. But she had pined for her native land, and before the marriage was a year old she had in desolate misery thrown herself from one of the long windows to the stone terrace far below.

Arabel, when a child, had sometimes peeped into the Chinese room, which was rarely occupied, and if nobody was about she tiptoed around, admiring the carved chests and bed and, above all, the silk paneling. How could the little bride from China have failed to be happy here, when through the love and thought of her husband it was as though part of her own country had been brought here also? But perhaps she had not loved him. Arabel knew nothing of the story except that she had been homesick, and that it was said her wraith had been seen standing by the window, gazing down at the terrace upon which her slender body had finally been broken.

Both Lady Thora and Mrs. Gibson had derided this ghostly story. Nobody in living memory had ever confessed to seeing this unhappy shade from the past, but such legends Lady Thora had said were invariably associated with old houses.

Arabel, however, on the night of her homecoming did not find it difficult to believe that something of that long-ago sorrow still lingered in the ornate room. She was herself oppressed by a brooding melancholy, which was natural since death had so recently claimed the mistress of Troy Court. Even when confined to her own rooms Lady Thora had made her presence felt, and Arabel was keenly conscious of loss. As yet she felt little elevation because she had so astonishingly stepped into Lady Thora's shoes. She was more preoccupied with her new understanding of her mother and the sense of the tremendous responsibilities that would be hers in the future. Could she possibly fit herself to such a position? Lady Thora had evidently believed so, and in any case it would be well over a year before she would be in real authority. During that time she would become acclimatized, she hoped, for she knew she was adaptable. At Seacrest College she had passed quite easily from pupil to teacher, had taken up new duties without sense of strain, and had been popular with both mistresses and girls. The latter had been largely owing to Charlotte Frewin, and she now thought of her with additional affection. Charlotte was so loyal and loving, had been so anxious that her departure should not mean a final rupture. Her tearstained face at the moment of parting was not easily to be forgotten.

There was no question now of becoming Charlotte's governess, though at the time it had seemed not impossible. She would have to write to Charlotte and tell her of the great change in her life.

From the schoolgirl who loved her, Arabel's thoughts passed to her half-brother. She had seen even less of Kit than of Lady Thora, but there had been a bond between them, though when they had last met she had been no more than a child, and he already a young man. Their encounters had been sparse, but Arabel cherished the memory of them.

She could not criticize the gentle Lady Thora because he had so rarely visited Troy Court. No embargo had been placed upon visits by her; it was the Herald uncle and aunt who were to blame, limiting the association between mother and son, to which fiat Ursula Gibson had been forced to agree for Kit's sake. He could, Arabel supposed, have set the Heralds at defiance of late years, but no doubt he was attached to them, and, since Lady Thora and Ursula had been more often abroad than at Troy Court, frequent meetings had been impossible.

Nor had it been possible for her to have any real homelife. Her mother had always been a wage earner, and Lady Thora's invalidism had made it impossible for her to indulge her affection for her children. Yet her main desire must have been for their security, and for this she had made great sacrifices. But these, Arabel decided, were in the past. Ursula had a right to the love and companionship of both her children; the Heralds could not prevent it, for money could make Kit independent of them. The fifteen months between now and her twenty-first birthday would soon pass.

This thought soothed Arabel's stunned and vaguely troubled spirit. She nestled down in the luxurious bed, and the hazy peace of approaching sleep passed over her in long, delicious waves. Soon she was blissfully unconscious.

# CHAPTER 3

Neither Mrs. Gibson nor Arabel received many personal letters, but a week after Arabel's departure from
Seacrest College a bulky envelope addressed in Charlotte's handwriting arrived for her. Within, there was a
long epistle, which spread over several sheets of writing
paper, and a group photograph, which had been taken
before Arabel left, of the senior pupils with Arabel in
the center. This photograph had been taken with the
intention of giving it to Miss Norton on her birthday,
suitably framed, but it had arrived too late for the day
and had been presented later. Charlotte wrote that she
was sure Arabel would wish to have a copy as a souvenir. She also wrote a good deal more. It was a touchingly
sincere and ingenuous letter. "I don't want to bore you
with expressions of affection," wrote Charlotte, "but
you meant something wonderfully special to me, and
you always will. Please write to me. Please let me know
if you will be at Troy Court for any length of time. If
so, we may meet sooner than I expected. My holiday
in France is postponed, for my relations over there have
all their children ill with whooping cough, and since I
have never had it my parents won't hear of my running
the risk. Besides, I should really be a nuisance, since I
have no experience of children or illness, and although
I would try to help I doubt if I should be of much use. I
was disappointed, but only for a short while, as I have

26

since been asked to spend the first part of the summer vacation with some cousins of mine who have recently bought a house within a few miles of you. It is called Green Lawns. My cousin is, or was, a physician. He has now given up his practice in Harley Street, but his son Nicholas, my second cousin, is taking it over, specializing in heart complaints—though not just yet, for on a holiday in Portugal he fell ill with typhoid fever, and although he has made a good recovery he will have to take things carefully for a while. I have accepted the invitation chiefly in the hope of seeing you, and, oh dear, I shall be bitterly disappointed if you have left the neighborhood by the time I arrive."

There was no fear of that, thought Arabel, as with a smile for its naïvety she glanced through the letter for a second time. Such heartfelt affection was heartwarming, and she decided she must answer Charlotte's letter by return, telling her of all that had happened and assuring her that she would look forward to meeting her again, not as a pupil but as a friend. After all, at sixteen, a girl who had had as much freedom as Charlotte and who had both originality and intelligence, was scarcely a child.

Mrs. Gibson came into the morning room where they usually breakfasted and stooped to pick up a page of Charlotte's letter which had fallen unnoticed to the ground. "A pretty handwriting," she commented. "I thought so when I looked through the post and left this letter beside your plate."

"I was dreadfully late this morning," Arabel apologized, but I slept badly. You must have had your breakfast ages ago. Bessie brought me fresh toast and coffee and a boiled egg as well."

"I rise early through long habit." Ursula sat down at the table. "When I had the responsibility of housekeeping, I found that the morning slipped away all too quickly. There was so much to do. Now I scarcely know how to fill my time. Is the coffee still hot?"

"Oh, yes, I haven't had mine yet. I stopped to read this letter." Arabel who knew that her mother could drink black coffee at any time, filled a cup and passed it to her. "It is from one of the pupils at Seacrest. I can hardly say *my* pupil, for I only taught the little ones, but it was one of my duties to sit at the desk in the sixth-form study room while the girls did their preparation or their needlework. It was extremely tedious. I couldn't read or occupy myself in any way, as I had to keep my eye on several of them. The mistresses all disliked this supervision duty and foisted it upon me as often as they could. These older girls were most of them so bored with the work, poor dears. They were all in their last year at the college and longing for it to be over."

"And yet school days are said to be the happiest in life," Mrs. Gibson commented. "I cannot vouch for it myself, though, as I had no education to speak of. That's something I bitterly regret, and I have done my best to overcome it by reading and visiting museums and picture galleries when Lady Thora and I were on the Continent."

"You must," said Arabel, "have learned a great deal more than anyone can learn from lesson books."

Pity stirred as she considered her mother's dogged perseverance. It was monstrous that the snobbish Heralds had despised her. She, in her mother's place, would have scorned *them,* would have kept her son with her, even if it had meant an inferior education and no possibility of professional status. Something of this she now said, but Ursula Gibson shook her head. "Wait until you are a mother yourself, my dear, then you will realize how natural it seems to put your children's welfare before your own."

Arabel doubted it and also doubted if anything could atone to a child for a virtually motherless childhood. How very unlike she and her mother were. She could scarcely imagine Ursula acting impetuously, but Arabel found cool discretion difficult. At Seacrest College she had acted a part, had been constantly on guard, for Miss Norton had preached propriety and self-control. Emotional friendships had been frowned upon, and it was really surprising that Charlotte's open devotion to her had not been criticized.

Even in appearance, Arabel bore no resemblance to her mother, and from out the mists of the past she recalled Lady Thora's comment on her likeness to her father.

"Did Lady Thora ever meet him?" she asked, and then, as her mother looked puzzled, "My father, I mean. Years ago I remember hearing her say I resembled him, but I think you said then that she was only referring to a portrait of him."

"She must have been. They never met."

"I have never seen that portrait, Ursula, and I should like to see it."

Mrs. Gibson sighed regretfully. "Unfortunately I have lost it, and it was the only one I ever possessed. For years I treasured it and it went with me on all my travels, but about a year ago I missed it. Some baggage was mislaid on our way to Vienna, and although it was finally recovered it had been ransacked, the contents replaced in confusion, and many items missing, of Lady Thora's as well as mine. This photograph in a frame was among them. It was a grief to me, though I am sure I showed it to you when you were a child."

"If you did, I don't remember it. Had he dark hair and green eyes as I have?"

"Yes—but not your pale skin—his was swarthy. Ours was a very short married life, as you know. It is sad to recall it."

"Was it a comfort to you to have me—a reminder of him?" Arabel asked, and then was sorry she had, as she saw her mother's healthy color fade to a leaden gray.

"Oh, my dear, if I am honest, I must confess that I was in such a confused and wretched state that I was

incapable of rational thought. It was a dreadful thing
to be widowed for the second time and with no provision made for me. But for Lady Thora I scarcely know
what I should have done. We were both grief-stricken,
for she was mourning her father. That helped to draw
us together. I only took service with her because I was
so lonely, having surrendered Kit, and being so much
separated from your father. I cannot say I particularly
wanted another child, but of course, when you were
actually here, both Lady Thora and I thought you
wonderful, and those first years when you were a little
thing were happy years."

"Well, now you will be much happier," Arabel promised. "It is sad that Lady Thora has gone, and we shall
never forget her or cease to be grateful, but she would
be glad that we can now be together. It will be wonderful to live here."

"Do not expect too much, Arabel. When it becomes
known that you have inherited the estate, many of the
big people hereabout may hold aloof, refuse to acknowl-
edge you as one of themselves. It would be a pity if that
made you bitter."

"It won't. If necessary we can do well enough without
such people. I shall not be without friends. This girl,
Charlotte Frewin, who has written to me, will soon be
visiting cousins in the neighborhood, and she seems
sure they will be delighted to know us, even though she
has no idea as yet that Troy Court has been bequeathed
to me. I ought to have written to her earlier to tell her."

"She knew my position here and it made no difference to her?" asked Ursula in surprise. "It would have
been much wiser to have told nobody at Seacrest College. I wonder Miss Norton did not insist on it. She
would never have taken you for a pupil but for Lady
Thora's persuasion. Who is this Miss Charlotte Frewin?
A lady?"

"Charlotte is a parlor boarder," said Arabel. "She is
an only daughter, rather spoiled but very sweet. Her

father is a baronet. I met him and Lady Frewin at last year's prizegiving. They were charming to me. I have no doubt they are rich, though at Seacrest one never speaks of money—to do so is considered bad taste: to complain if one is poor, or to boast if one is rich. I only told Charlotte my circumstances because, although she is three years younger, we became especially friendly. She would never have settled down at Seacrest but that she attached herself to me."

"Really? Where does she live and who are her cousins here?"

"Her home is at Bellbridge. Her cousins have recently bought a house called Green Lawns. She doesn't mention their name but says her cousin is, or was, a Harley Street physician, and that his son Nicholas is also a doctor. But read her letter for yourself."

Mrs. Gibson glanced swiftly through the pages handed to her. "She certainly seems very fond of you," she commented. "When driving I have passed this residence, Green Lawns. It is a pretty place—commodious, but not one of the great houses. It may be an advantage to you socially if these people take you up."

"I wish we need not think in that way."

"It is the way the world thinks, my dear, and you will be sensible to accept it, for otherwise you will be lonely. I would not for anything stand in your light, and it has occurred to me that you might do better with a hired duenna, some lady of small means but high connections. There is no compulsion for me to live here, a drawback to you."

"How can you speak so? It's a dreadful suggestion—almost an insult to me."

"An insult?"

"To suggest I am so horrible, so unnatural, as to be ashamed of you because you worked for your living." Arabel rose and put her arms round her mother. "Never say such a thing again."

"Very well." Ursula's lips lightly touched Arabel's

cheek. "We can go on as we are for the time being. Later, when you marry, there are bound to be changes."

"Not necessarily, and, as I have said before, I have no inclination toward marriage."

Ursula smiled, shook her head with tolerant disbelief, and withdrew herself from her daughter's embrace. Arabel was conscious of disappointment. She sensed a lack of warmth, and it was as though her mother humored her as she might have humored a child, unaware of her longing for the tender intimacy that had been denied her. They had grown too far apart, Arabel supposed, and she could only hope that time would draw them together.

Mrs. Gibson glanced at the clock and said, "You have an appointment with Mr. Brecknell this morning. Eleven o'clock at his office. Had you forgotten? Since he was away it was better, I thought, to wait to see him instead of his partner."

"I hadn't forgotten." Arabel spoke indifferently, for she was still feeling deflated.

"The carriage has been ordered for a quarter past ten. It takes over half an hour to drive into Storkley."

"You will come with me, won't you?"

"If you wish, but Mr. Brecknell's business is with you, not me. He will make everything clear to you, and for an interview with your lawyer, who is at least sixty, a chaperon is scarcely necessary."

"No, but I *want* you to be with me. There is nothing to keep you at home this morning."

"And that is a very peculiar feeling. I was quite lost each time I returned with Lady Thora from Europe. Margaret Harris had everything under control and had no need of me, yet for years there was no domestic detail which was not referred to me."

"Would you be happier without Mrs. Harris? I don't want you to raise a finger, but if you feel so lost, so aimless . . . she could be paid off, couldn't she? You could have a couple of young maids to train in place of her, who would act as underhousekeepers."

Mrs. Gibson shrugged as though the matter was not, after all, of particular importance. "It would be a great blow to Margaret Harris were she to be dismissed, and she has done nothing to deserve it. It would be better to leave things as they are for now." She glanced at the clock. "If you wish me to accompany you, I must change from this dress to something more suitable. And you must do the same, my dear."

Mr. Sydney Brecknell, of Brecknell, Daytown, and Crest, was a dapper sixty. He wore a gray suit which was much the same tinge as his skin, there was a fine pearl in his tiepin, and a heavy gold watch chain with a dangling fob. Smiling at Arabel, he remarked that when she was a very small girl she had been wont to sit on his knee and play with it. She had found the little pocket where his watch was lodged and had held it up to her ear to listen to its ticking. "In those early days," he said, "Lady Thora liked to have you with her as much as possible."

Mrs. Gibson remembered and agreed. "So she did. She was very fond of small children, and Arabel was spoiled. She was considered very wayward when she first went to the village school."

"She has grown up to be a most stately young lady." Mr. Brecknell's gaze was discreetly admiring. "It is not to be wondered at that dear Lady Thora had so much affection for her, and she was certainly one to indulge her fancies. Why she went to a strange lawyer in London to draw up this will, while at the same time making me the executor, is a mystery. Could she have feared I should endeavor to dissuade her? Far from it. She has made a reasonable disposition of her property, instead of the peculiar bequests she insisted upon twenty years before. I know my poor father was much put about over it, and rightly, for nearly all those obscure organizations have since vanished into limbo. The administration of her estate, had there been no later will, would have been a problem. Troy Court would have come under the hammer for one thing, and speaking unofficially I sincerely hope that this, Miss Gibson, is not in your mind."

Arabel said, "I should be brokenhearted to sell Troy Court."

"And you, Mrs. Gibson, feel the same?"

Ursula raised her brows in surprise. "The decision does not rest with me, Mr. Brecknell."

"Ah, there you are mistaken. Is it possible you have not understood . . . ?"

"What *is* there to understand?" Ursula's calm was shaken. There was a roughness in her voice which betrayed her peasant origin.

"I fully believe that my partner had made it clear to you that should your daughter die before attaining the age of twenty-one, all that has been bequeathed to her reverts to you."

"Oh no!" The exclamation was involuntary, and, as once before, Arabel saw a gray shade steal over her mother's face. This leaden tinge strangely altered the familiar aspect, and she wondered anxiously if her mother were really as strong, as healthy, as she normally appeared.

"Do not distress yourself," the lawyer advised soothingly. "It is, after all, an unlikely contingency, but in law every contingency has to be considered, and this no doubt was pointed out to Lady Thora when the terms of this second will were discussed. You, at the present moment, are your daughter's heir and Lady Thora's second choice. Should Miss Gibson meet with an untimely end, you would be the sole beneficiary. She cannot, before attaining her majority, divert this fortune elsewhere, even if she would."

Mrs. Gibson swallowed convulsively, and it was a few moments before she could speak; when she did it

was in a low voice. "I certainly had no idea of this . . .
I did not think of it . . . if I had, I suppose I should
have taken it for granted that Lady Thora's distant Irish
relations would benefit. But I refuse to consider anything so dreadful. In a little less than fifteen months,
Arabel will be in full control, will she not?"

"Certainly she will, and much can happen in that
time—the prospect of marriage and a family, for one
thing. My dear Mrs. Gibson, I regret to have so distressed you. Would you perhaps care for a glass of
wine?"

Ursula refused with a shake of the head and a murmur of thanks. She was foolish, but this clause in the
will had come as a shock to her, and it was terrible to
speak of death in connection with Arabel. She sought
for her handkerchief and, finding it, pressed it to her
eyes. Arabel was moved. She put out her hand and Mrs.
Gibson clasped it. Mr. Brecknell smiled at them over
his glinting spectacles. It was, he thought, a pleasant
thing to see so much affection between a mother and
daughter. His own daughter, recently married, had constantly squabbled with him and his wife, and they had
been thankful to have her settled.


Although a copy of the will was duly sent to Arabel,
she put it aside and did not glance at it, for the day
after the visit to the lawyer's office she was out walking
in the woods that adjoined Troy Court, when rain
descended in an unexpected torrent. Arabel was wearing a thin summer dress, which did not prevent her
from making for the house instead of sheltering beneath
the trees, with the result that she was drenched to the
skin. Although she changed at once, she was, a few
hours later, shivering miserably, and her mother persuaded her to go to bed and have her evening meal
brought to her there on a tray.

"But I hardly ever catch cold," she protested. "I'm

as strong as a horse—which was a great advantage at Seacrest, for I was always available to take on extra duties if a mistress was ill."

"It does seem as though they took advantage of you there," said Mrs. Gibson. "If I had suspected it, I should have worried, for I doubt if you're as strong as you think; for one thing you are too thin. A little spoiling won't hurt you, and will be quite a pleasure to me as I've never had the chance to spoil you."

The chance to spoil! But surely there had been many such chances. Dimly, for it must have been far back in her early childhood, Arabel recalled instances of impetuous affection which had been repelled. She must once have longed to be demonstrative but for years had known better than to betray it. A child could be hurt and yet give no sign, could remember clutching at a skirt or apron with small fingers, probably grubby, which had been decisively dislodged.

A fall, resulting in a grazed knee, had been an occasion for scolding, not consolation; a face upturned from the pillow for a good-night kiss, had been ignored.

Fever, instead of clouding, appeared now to heighten Arabel's perception. She hated herself for doubting, yet she did doubt a maternal love that had forbidden the gift of a kitten, whose acceptance Lady Thora would certainly have allowed—that had failed to alleviate long, lonely hours when she had had childish complaints such as measles and whooping cough. It was Lady Thora who had been anxious about her and who had sent books and games, though forbidden by the doctor to visit her for fear of infection.

"You're so different now," Arabel said impulsively. Mrs. Gibson, about to leave the room, turned abruptly to gaze at her. "In what way?"

"Softer." Arabel made an effort to assemble her thoughts. "Seeming to need me. I could never persuade myself that you did. We . . . I . . . when I put my arms round you the other day and you permitted it, I felt . . .

strange, shy almost, as though I had no right and you might resent it."

"Oh, my dear!" The older woman's fresh, kindly face puckered in distress. "How easy it is for people to misunderstand each other. My position was a difficult one, and I had theories about rearing a child who would, when grown, have to support herself. I was determined that you should be independent, that I would not cling to you, be a burden to you. It's only now that I can dare to show—to show . . ."

Her voice trembled. Arabel was aghast. She moved quickly forward, but Mrs. Gibson said hastily, "Dearest child, you must give me time. I am so accustomed to suppress all I feel . . ."

She hurried from the room, and Arabel's mind whirled. It was she who was to blame, not perhaps when she was a child but certainly since she had grown-up. She ought to have fathomed the restraint that Ursula had put upon herself, ought to have suspected the un-selfish motive. Now her mother's near breakdown into tears had convinced her. Arabel had not believed her capable of such emotion.

The glowing fire in the Chinese room flickered on the walls and caused the birds, flowers, and figures to start into life. Rain splashed against the window. When Mrs. Gibson returned, her face was as placid, her manner as calm as usual, and neither of them alluded to the few moments before when she had not been so calm. Arabel was helped to undress and tucked into bed with a hot brick against her cold feet. Mrs. Gibson brought her a tisane which she had brewed herself. It was, she said, better than any doctor's medicine for a chill. Lady Thora had had great faith in her homemade remedies. Arabel sipped the steaming herbal brew and found it agreeable with its spicy taste and odor. "Did you invent it yourself?" she asked.

"Dear me, no! It is a recipe from a very old collection of herbal remedies—not printed, but copied out by one of the ladies of the family who lived about two hundred years ago. I found it soon after I came here, when I was turning out the contents of an old chest, hunting for some trifle Lady Thora had mislaid and wanted. I expect these homely cures were handed down by word of mouth, until somebody took the trouble to write them down for the benefit of the household. Some are cures for illnesses unknown in these times, but most are for chills, sore throats, and coughs, migraine, sleeplessness, and the like."

"I haven't slept at all well lately," Arabel confided. "All the excitement, probably. Over and over again I dream it is a mistake, that Troy Court doesn't really belong to me, that some near relation arrives and I have to give it up."

"You heard Mr. Brecknell say that those distant Irish cousins had no claim, and there are no nearer relations. The excited feeling will wear off before long, and you will take your inheritance for granted."

"Perhaps." The figures on the panels danced before Arabel's feverish eyes. "This is not a restful room, Ursula. It's beautiful, but there is too much color—it is too grand. I would far rather have the little room in the West Tower that I had as a child."

"Oh Arabel, surely not! It was all very well for a child, but it would never do for the mistress of the house —so small and comfortless in comparison with this. Really there *is* no other suite suitable for you just yet. We agreed that Lady Thora's should be entirely redecorated and repainted and have fresh covers made for the chairs, and I am doing my best to hurry on the workmen, but they are so laggardly. However, in a few weeks, if you wish to change, that suite will be ready for you."

Arabel sighed, but was too tired to argue further. Her mother was obviously resolved that she should be given the utmost importance; perhaps Ursula was oversensitive, fearing that the servants might at the least excuse treat the new mistress of Troy Court with disrespect. Arabel thought better of them. So far as she could judge, every member of the staff, from the housekeeper to the youngest housemaid, seemed anxious to please, but Ursula might know better. Reluctantly she gave in.

"Oh well, I can put up with Oriental splendor for a few weeks, though I can't forget that this room has tragic associations."

"But my dear, so many years ago. Various visitors have slept here since and nobody ever complained. On the contrary, they praised the comfort and convenience and admired the beautiful silk panels."

"Well, so do I, of course, but . . ."

"You must have a soothing tisane each night, and then you will sleep soundly."

Arabel said no more, and she did sleep well that night. Her cold kept her in bed for a few days, and she became accustomed to the panorama of the Chinese landscape, which, when the windows were slightly open, quivered and moved as though with an individual life. Nonetheless she was extremely glad when she was able to get up and go downstairs.

While in bed she had been able to write letters, and she had replied to Charlotte's with a warmth which she knew would give delight. It was a genuine warmth, for she was really longing for their next meeting. This somewhat surprised her, for at Seacrest College it was Charlotte who was forlorn unless they frequently saw each other; but Arabel had not been lonely then, and although she had her mother's company, she was often lonely now. As Ursula had warned, few people called on them—only Mrs. Galbraith, the doctor's wife, and the vicar's sister, who kept house for him, he being an elderly and childless widower. Lady Thora, gentle and kind though she was, would not have considered that these worthy ladies were her social equals, but to Arabel and her mother their attitude was slightly condescending, which annoyed Ursula considerably.

"Let us hope," she said, "that when your friend Charlotte Frewin arrives, it will make a difference. These cousins of hers can scarcely be known in the neighborhood as yet, but I heard the other day—I think it was when I was chatting with Mrs. Brecknell, who called while you were still confined to your room—that Charlotte's parents are friendly with the Wentworths at the Tower House. They—or rather she—are immensely rich—an American who brought her husband a fortune."

"Does that really count in such a neighborhood as this? I mean it seems to be old families, preferably titled ones, that are important here."

"Tony Wentworth was in the Guards and he is connected with some of the finest families, but even if he were a parvenu, money on the Wentworth scale would count anywhere," Mrs. Gibson commented dryly. "Cosette Wentworth's parents brought her over for the London season, and it is said she could have married a duke. I believe her family were very disappointed when she fell in love with Captain Wentworth. However, the marriage seems to have turned out very well. Tower House was falling into ruins, but her money has restored it, and he gave up his commission and settled down as a landowner. They are said to be very happily matched and now have three children. They entertain on a magnificent scale. Doubtless your young friend will be calling on them, or they on her, and she will tell them that you were her school friend."

"Hardly that. Charlotte did not come to Seacrest until I was a pupil teacher there. Her fondness for me may be no more than a schoolgirl's infatuation. It alleviated her hatred of a boarding school. I doubt if she will stay long at Seacrest now that I have gone. Her parents are very indulgent and will allow her to leave if she is unhappy. Charlotte thought she could persuade them to engage me as her private governess, though of course that is impossible now as she will realize when she receives my letter."

"She will probably want you to go on a visit to her, but if so, I hope you will put her off for a while. I feel I am only just beginning to get to know you—my own daughter."

"I feel the same, and I should hate to leave Troy Court so soon. . . ."

Arabel broke off. The velvet *portière* stirred slightly as though by a gust of wind. The door was ajar, otherwise they would not have heard the slight commotion in the hall, the opening and closing of the front door, and then a voice, a man's voice, unknown to Arabel but evidently familiar to Ursula, who rose with a swift exclamation, casting aside the embroidery work which generally employed her busy fingers when she and Arabel talked together.

She went swiftly to the sitting room door and flung it wide, her face irradiated. She said, "It's Kit." Arabel also rose, her heart fluttering. Five years ago when she had last seen her half-brother, he had seemed little more than an overgrown boy, but by now he must surely be much changed. How extraordinary to have a brother who was a stranger! And why hadn't he given them warning of this visit?

Mrs. Gibson returned with her hand linked in the arm of a tall, young man, slimly built save for his broad shoulders. He had matured, but not changed so much after all. Arabel recalled the shock of fair hair, the pointed chin, and wide-set gray eyes.

"Such a surprise!" Mrs. Gibson was divided between delight and agitation. Her cheeks were flushed. She looked at least ten years younger. "My dearest boy, why didn't you write to tell me?"

"Impulse," said Kit. "When I received your last letter, I decided I must see you both—stay for a while, if you can put up with me."

"*Put up with you!* You know very well . . . I was

afraid to suggest it, not knowing how Edmund and Grace would take it."

He shrugged. "They know the time has gone by when they could raise objections." He met Arabel's eyes and smiled at her. "Sometimes I could scarcely believe I possessed a sister, and I certainly couldn't imagine you grown up, Bel. The picture I had in my mind was of a little dark girl with a pigtail—all legs and arms and skinny. . . ."

Against her will, Arabel was tongue-tied. His easy use of the pet name he had given her when she was a child moved her heart. Mrs. Gibson said, "Arabel is still too thin, and she has been ill just lately, her resistance lowered I am sure by shock. As you will realize, dearest, her life has been turned upside down."

"But wasn't that exhilarating?" Kit asked. He crossed the room to Arabel, took her hand, stooped slightly to kiss her cheek. "Say you are pleased to see me." His voice was coaxing.

"But of course, of course I am. Pleased is a poor word to describe . . ." The air seemed to vibrate between them. Arabel's nerves tingled. She uttered a small, broken laugh, but she could just as easily have wept. "This is a wonderful moment," she said, and added perfunctorily, "especially for Ursula."

"Wonderful for all three of us. We're a family at last," said Kit.

# CHAPTER 4

The first weeks following Lady Thora's death had been confused and unreal, but with Kit's advent everything became vivid and clear-cut. Ursula was so reserved as to seem at times almost inarticulate, but under Kit's influence she expanded. He charmed and amused her, was openly affectionate, complimented her on her looks, evinced a genuine pride in her. Ursula's formal graciousness, her agreeable but somewhat fixed smile were replaced by laughter and a relaxed happiness. Kit and his mother were so much together that sometimes Arabel felt shut out. The intimacy they had been slowly building up was at a standstill, if not shattered.

She guessed that Kit would willingly have spent more time with her, but Ursula's possessiveness was difficult to set aside, and for the first week she rarely left them together. This passed swiftly. Nothing was said to indicate the intended length of Kit's stay; no letters arrived for him from his uncle or aunt, and at last Mrs. Gibson, egged on by curiosity, alluded to this.

"They can't write, because they don't know I am here," said Kit. "They may suspect it, but, being on such frosty terms with you, they would rather endure suspense than write to make inquiries, much less pay a personal visit to discover if I have taken refuge with you."

43

"Refuge?" echoed Mrs. Gibson. "Do you need a refuge?"

"Well . . . yes, and I hoped to find it with you and Arabel."

"Kit, have you done anything you should not have done?"

He laughed. "Any amount of things, my dear Mamma."

It was evening, Arabel at the piano in the drawing room had been playing softly, but now her hands fell from the keyboard. She rose from the piano stool, she stood hesitantly, prepared to leave Ursula and Kit together, but Kit, glancing at her, said, "Come and sit over here, Bel. I should have spoken out before, but I always shirk serious conversations and to be here with you both was so enjoyable."

Mrs. Gibson drew her skirts aside to make room for Arabel on the settee beside her. She smiled at her absently, all her real attention concentrated on her son.

Arabel hesitated. In spite of her mother's gesture and Kit's invitation, she still felt that she was the unwanted third. "If there is anything wrong, wouldn't you prefer to discuss it alone?" she suggested.

"There's nothing wrong in the sense of disgrace or dishonor," Kit replied impatiently, "and what I have to tell concerns you as much as it concerns Mother—more, perhaps, as this is, strictly speaking, your property."

"That hasn't sunk in yet. I still feel I am on a visit here."

"Nonetheless, if you don't want me here, Bel, and say so, Mother cannot overrule you."

"Of course I want you here. Why are you being so mysterious?"

"Heaven only knows. I'm a bit on edge, I dare say. I hadn't an idea how either of you would take it, if I told you that I had broken with my uncle and aunt. That's been pending for months—for years, though when the final crash came it was sudden."

Ursula's face wore a stunned expression. She was too startled to feel immediate elation. "But you never hinted at it, only wrote once or twice in your letters that you found reading law a boring business, but that you had a sideline in which you were interested. How can you break with them when they have done so much for you?"

"Wasn't that to please themselves as much as to benefit me?"

"I don't know—how should I know? But your education has been expensive, and these last three years at Cambridge, you have worked hard to get your degree. Why—if your heart wasn't in it?"

"I owed Uncle Edmund that much. I warned him before going up to Cambridge that he might be wasting his money. I told him that law bored me to such an extent I might go out of my mind if it was to be my destiny. He refused to take me seriously. I have a flair, some people have, for passing examinations, and so had done well at school. At Cambridge I've taken a First. Uncle Edmund wrung a promise from me that I would work and work hard. He said it would be time enough to settle my future when I had my degree. Well, I gave my promise and kept it, and I suppose he thought I had overcome what to him was no more than boyish rebellion. When I broke it to him and Aunt Grace that I had not changed by so much as an iota, there was a storm. That night I packed my bags and left—by stealth, I suppose you might say, though I made no real attempt to avoid noise. I left a letter saying that whatever happened I should not return."

Arabel said, "But it doesn't seem like you to be so ruthless, especially to people you were fond of."

"Ah, but that's the thing, Bel—I'm not fond of them and never have been. It's very different to feel a forced gratitude for a home, clothes, a good education—and I suppose I should say an adequate allowance, though I discovered that Mother provided the greater part of that. I went to Cambridge against my will, and I can't be sure if either of them were really fond of me."

"My dear, of course they were," said Mrs. Gibson with a dragging reluctance. "Your aunt was childless— it must have been a grief to her. Years ago they gave me no peace until I agreed to hand you over to them. It angered them that I refused to surrender you to the extent of never seeing you, never writing to you. I couldn't bring myself to that, even for your sake."

"I'm thankful you didn't. At least I knew you were there in the background. I can't remember the time when I didn't resent their attitude to you—one of contempt, because according to them you were socially no credit to the precious family. I've often thought that what they did was as much to hurt you as for any love of me, though there was also pride. I was a Herald, and as such must carry on the family business. When I decided to leave forever, I admit I hoped you would give me houseroom. Lady Thora was a kind soul and wouldn't have grudged it, and I needed a few weeks in a peaceful retreat."

"But of course you can stay here for as long as you choose." Ursula Gibson spoke with confidence, yet at the same time glanced inquiringly at Arabel. "That is, if your sister . . . ?"

"I'll be delighted," Arabel said promptly. "Apart from which, Ursula, I feel and always shall feel that Troy Court is as much yours as mine."

"My dear, doesn't it occur to you that this great house would be a burden, an encumbrance to me? I have given the best years of my life to it, was paid to do so, but have never felt inclined to say as you did when you were a child that it is the most beautiful place in all the world, that I loved it and thought of it as the perfect home. That counted with Lady Thora and she remembered it; more than once throughout the years she spoke of it."

"And you think that is why the place and Lady

Thora's fortune were left to Bel?" Kit's smile flashed amusement.

"Yes, I do."

"Few innocently childish words of praise can have paid such high dividends."

"There was affection as well," Ursula said. "Arabel endeared herself to Lady Thora. She thought her a splendid girl and took the greatest interest in her. But I dare say she would have taken an equal interest in you, Kit, had it been possible for you to come here oftener. I wish . . ."

She broke off, evidently fearing that, drawn out of her habitual reserve, she had said too much.

"You wish that I had been given a share of this inheritance? But I have, or shall have, I hope and believe, no need of it. Now is the moment for confession. My dear, sweet Mamma, I am not exactly penniless. I have written a book, a novel, which was accepted a few months ago and will be published in the autumn. I have started upon another. That's the career I chose years ago, though I had to practice, to experiment, to destroy nearly everything I wrote—appalling efforts they were too. But during my first year at Cambridge, I had a few short stories accepted. One appeared in the *Cornhill*, others in less famous journals. Don't gape at me like that, Bel. Didn't I invent stories for you years ago when you were avid for them?"

"Yes, you did, but how could I imagine you seriously intended to be a writer? Why didn't you tell Ursula? Why didn't you send her copies of the stories that were published?"

"Because I wasn't sure of myself, or of the worth of such talent as I have. The stories were written under a pseudonym, but the book will be published under my own name."

"How *could* you find the time when you were working for a degree?" Ursula asked, staring at him as she might have stared with wonder had all the great marvels of the universe been spread before her eyes.

He shrugged. "Didn't I say just now that some people have a useful flair for passing examinations without much difficulty, and that I am one of them? It's a superficial talent, for, once having acquired information, I don't remember it for any length of time."

"It is what is called a photographic memory," said Arabel.

"Exactly. Do you also possess it, Bel?"

"No, I have to slog. Nobody has ever said I was brilliant."

"Just as well, perhaps; few men are attracted to clever women."

This was an observation warranted to arouse ire, and Arabel said haughtily, "I only wish I *were* brilliant, what is called a bluestocking. I'd far rather be that than a pretty fool, cultivating beguiling tricks in order to win a husband."

Kit burst out laughing. "My sweet, with your fortune you need no such wiles. You'll be a glittering prize for any fortune hunter—a danger which must already have occurred to Mother, if not to you."

A flicker—was it of anxiety?—crossed Ursula's face. "Arabel assures me that she is not attracted by the thought of marriage, and she is, I am convinced, too sensible to rush into one.

"At nineteen," said Kit, "there is certainly no hurry for it, and why shouldn't you enjoy your freedom for a while? But men have their uses, if only as escorts, and, when you and Mamma emerge from the seclusion of mourning, I can act as such."

"It's unlikely that we shall receive many invitations. Nobody of social importance seems to be aware of our existence."

"But these are early days, Bel. Lady Thora's death is recent, and although you were not related to her, as her heiress you are expected to be in temporary retirement.

However, as it happens, I have a few acquaintances living in this district, people I met on a trip abroad during vacation last summer. They were agreeable people and asked me to contact them should I ever be in these parts. I told them it was unlikely, and, although my mother was Lady Thora's companion-housekeeper, they were rarely here, owing to Lady Thora's prolonged sojourns at spas and foreign clinics."

"Who were they?" asked Mrs. Gibson.

"I have a card somewhere. Wentworth is the name."

"That is quite a coincidence. Arabel has a friend, a girl educated at Seacrest College, who is also friendly with the Wentworths. They are a family of importance, and just before you arrived I was telling Arabel about them. She has the money, but he has the social position."

"I heard all about that," said Kit. "Cosette Wentworth said that, although received by the local elite, she was, for a time, held at arm's length, as she was thought to have bought her way into society. This struck her as laughable as she had made such a triumphant London debut."

"The old county families are very stiff and proud," Mrs. Gibson said. "Many consider themselves more important than royalty. It's not to be wondered at, perhaps, as they can trace descent to before the Norman Conquest. However, the trend is now toward democracy, for which the late Prince Consort is said to be responsible. Irrespective of birth, he had the greatest respect for men of learning."

"Are your books learned, Kit?" asked Arabel.

"I wouldn't say so. My vein is considerably lighter than Scott or Thackeray. But the books do entail considerable research—that is why the peace of this place and a fine library in which to browse will be of the greatest value. The novel to be published in the autumn deals chiefly with the Titus Oates episode, and the one I am now working on is set in the region of Queen

Anne. If I had my way, I should have read for a history degree, not for law."

"How interested Lady Thora would have been," sighed his mother. "She had a veneration for writers, derived no doubt from Lord Riba, who thought it an honor to have shaken Charles Dickens by the hand. His books are all in the library—first editions. If Arabel agrees, the room could be set aside for you, as we seldom use it."

Arabel said thoughtfully. "It might be even better to turn one of the unoccupied rooms into a study for Kit. If—later—we have guests staying here, we cannot bar them from the library. But Kit, when working, could lock himself away in a room of his own and still make full use of the library."

"A good idea," her mother allowed.

"But it will be putting you to a lot of trouble for what may be only a short stay," Kit objected. "The refuge I need is temporary. A man I know has chambers in Bloomsbury, and in the autumn he is going to Australia and has agreed to sublet them to me."

"But that is weeks ahead," said Mrs. Gibson, "and to prepare a study for you will be no trouble at all. I must say, though, that I shall be surprised if we do have guests to stay."

A plan newly conceived had already taken root in Arabel's mind, and this seemed the opportunity to speak of it. "I am not so sure. There is Charlotte. Although her education is by no means complete, I feel convinced she has no intention of returning to Seacrest College. I told you how anxious she was I should act as her governess, and I see no reason why I should altogether disappoint her."

Mrs. Gibson gazed at her aghast. "But that is absurd. A governess! You—with your altered status!"

"I can't be her governess, certainly, but if her parents approve I can ask her to stay here and can supervise her studies. Why not? It would be possible for her to have visiting masters to instruct in foreign languages and music and drawing. I shall suggest this to her."

"Why, Bel, are you so fond of teaching?" Kit teased. "You haven't the look of a typical schoolmarm."

"And what look is that supposed to be?" For no reason at all Arabel was affronted, and her eyes flashed.

There was a corresponding flash in Kit's, but his was of admiration. Ursula was staring at her as though she had suddenly become a stranger.

"You know very well—sallow skin, hair strained away from a high, intellectual, knobby forehead, spectacles, and a prim mouth. Dress, uniformly severe, tight to the neck and the wrists and of a drab shade, if not of unrelieved black."

"Well, I am wearing black of necessity, and my forehead is high except that my hair curls over it." A smile broke forth as she glanced down at her crinoline, which no governess would have been permitted to wear. The spreading skirts were of a fine silk muslin, ornamented by a profusion of black velvet bows. From the day of her arrival at Troy Court, a dressmaker already engaged by Mrs. Gibson had been installed in the sewing room, working long hours each day to augment a sparse wardrobe. Mrs. Gibson remarked with satisfaction that although girls with hair as dark as Arabel's did not usually look well in black, she, because of her green eyes and magnolia skin, was not dimmed by it. "I would not say I was fond of teaching," Arabel now admitted, "but I am very fond of Charlotte. I should enjoy having her here for a long visit, and I do not believe that would be possible unless I promised to see that her education was not neglected."

Ursula, though far from approving, made no further objection. It was possible that this absurd plan would come to nothing. Charlotte Frewin's parents would probably object, would insist, whatever Arabel might say and Charlotte wish, on their daughter returning to Seacrest College. Arabel, who knew better, did not enlarge on the spoiled girl's domination over doting parents. If Charlotte wanted to stay indefinitely at Troy Court, then Charlotte would, and Arabel was glad that this random idea had floated into her mind. Three was an awkward number, four was a comfortable one.

"You are a creature of surprises," Kit said the following day.

Ursula had driven into Spurbottle, the nearest town, in order to buy a new carpet, rugs, and a suitable desk and swivel chair for the room which had already been stripped of its bedroom furniture. Delighted to be preparing this room for her son, she had gone into action. The servants had been given orders that entailed extra work, and not for the first time Margaret Harris pursed a disapproving mouth. To serve Lady Thora was well enough, to serve the former housekeeper quite another.

Sometimes Margaret wished she had given her notice on Lady Thora's death, for she and Ursula Gibson had never been congenial. Lady Thora was different. It had been impossible not to like her, not to pity her.

Margaret, alone in the world, a childless widow, had been touched, startled, grateful when told of the legacy Lady Thora had left her, and with regard to this bequest Ursula had been surprisingly pleasant, assuring Margaret that she was delighted, that the legacy had been well deserved, and saying that she hoped Margaret would stay on as housekeeper. The fewer changes the better, Ursula had said, and she felt sure her daughter, now mistress of Troy Court, would endorse this.

Margaret had agreed, knowing that such a good situation was to be valued. Ursula had said that she expected her daughter to see fit, in consideration of Margaret's greater responsibility, to raise her salary. Now, having observed Arabel for a while, Margaret realized that Ursula was still likely to be the real mistress, for hadn't this been so in Lady Thora's lifetime? She had then been in full control, and it was improbable that a girl of nineteen, bewildered by her new wealth and status, would not rely completely on her capable mother.

Margaret's salary *had* been raised, so had the salary of several others, but oddly, Ursula was not popular, though the servants knew that the extra money was due to her suggestion. She was obeyed, respected, but not liked—she never had been. Margaret would have said she was far from fanciful, but there was something about the present state of affairs that depressed her. None of the staff had seen much of Arabel in Lady Thora's lifetime; her visits had been brief and sparse.

Rolt, the senior footman, had given it as his opinion that Duchess Ursula, as she was ironically called, cared little for her daughter, though Lady Thora had been inclined to make a pet of her. But her son, now, by a first marriage, he was different. Sometimes it was as though the Duchess for all her high and mighty ways *had* to talk about him, to boast of his good looks and his talent. A weak spot he was, said Rolt.

Margaret didn't blame Ursula for this. Mr. Kit was as nice as could be, handsome but didn't put on airs, was naturally considerate. Any mother would have been proud of him, would have doted on him. But Margaret did not for a moment believe that Ursula had the same kind of affection for Arabel. She put on a lot, of course —it was dearest this, and darling that, and such a constant fuss about her health, but none of it was convincing. Once or twice Margaret had seen a look in her eyes . . . .

Resolutely, Margaret endeavored to stifle criticism and dislike of her employer, which Ursula virtually was. The room designed to be Kit's study had to be cleared out, altered and prepared to receive fresh furniture within twenty-four hours, and it was none of Margaret's business, even if she did suspect that Arabel was the object of her mother's envy and resentment. It was absurd to feel so profoundly that a dark cloud now hovered over Troy Court.

Kit and Arabel had both been invited to drive into Spurbottle with Ursula. Both had made excuses which had been graciously accepted. Ursula enjoyed shopping and really preferred to do so alone. Arabel had said that Miss Tiller in the sewing room had asked her to try on two new dresses that were almost finished. She had added that she might possibly fill in the rest of the time by washing her hair. Kit had unpacked the manuscript he was working on and intended to revise the first chapters, the library being at his disposal.

Arabel duly tried on the two dresses, signified her approval, and then, as the afternoon was fine and sunny, decided that the shampooing of her hair could be left until the next day. It was the first time that her mother had gone beyond the grounds of Troy Court without her.

Now she was surprised to find how pleasant it was to be alone for a short while. It was sometimes a strain to bear with Ursula's watchful concern over her health. This had always been excellent, and it surely wasn't extraordinary that, having been drenched in a thunderstorm, she had contracted a bad chill, which might, if she had not taken care, have developed into pleurisy or pneumonia.

But she *had* taken care. She had gone to bed, had obediently swallowed the pills and medicines prescribed by Dr. Galbraith, with the additional tisanes brewed by Ursula of which he knew nothing. The chill, thus treated, had soon been vanquished, though in spite of the tisanes she did not sleep well, and for that reason, no doubt, often felt vague and dreamy during the daytime.

Hitherto it had not occurred to Arabel that she was as much irked as touched by her mother's concern for her. Even on this warm and sunny day Ursula would probably have hurried after her with an unwanted wrap when she stepped out upon the terrace, although she wouldn't have pressed her company upon Arabel—not now that Kit was at Troy Court. He, as yet, had had little opportunity to work on his book, but Ursula was not to blame for that, since she had known nothing about it until the previous day. How proud Ursula was of Kit, and what an immense satisfaction it was to her that he had discarded the Heralds. She had behaved well over this, had said nothing in complaint of their treatment of her. Instead she had urged Kit to write to his uncle, telling him where he was, thanking him for all he had done in the past, and explaining that he intended to devote himself to a literary career. The Heralds now could do nothing to hamper him.

Arabel descended the stone steps that led from the terrace and, the sun being bright, unfurled her parasol, which was of white lace lined with pink silk. It had belonged to Lady Thora, and Arabel sighed as she remembered this. She owed such an incredible amount to that gentle, sweet woman. Was it perhaps a pity that Lady Thora *had* been quite so gentle, a pity she had not insisted Arabel should leave Seacrest College instead of becoming a pupil teacher there? This was what she must have wanted, and Ursula would have consented had she said that she intended to make Arabel her heiress. As it was, Ursula was not to blame for ignoring a wish only wistfully suggested, for she had believed she was securing her daughter's future.

It was perplexing to reflect that for all her gentleness, Lady Thora had been devious. Why had she seized the opportunity when in London, with Ursula absent on a shopping jaunt, to consult a strange solicitor? This could not have been an impulsive action; there must have been letters of instruction sent privately when she was abroad, letters which had not been entrusted to Ursula to post. There was something disturbing about such stealth. Had she expected Ursula to raise objections which she was determined to avoid? But, in the second will, Ursula's legacy had been more than tripled.

Kit's voice broke in upon her reverie. He called to her as she walked across the lawn. "I saw you from the library window. What a glorious afternoon, and there are too few of them to waste in a so-called English summer. I can work this evening."

"Can you—just like that? Put down your pen in the middle of writing an exciting scene and pick it up hours later to continue without any sense of lost inspiration?" Arabel waited for him to join her and they strolled together toward the rose garden, which in turn led to the tennis courts. They were alone, as they had not been alone since his arrival.

"I've never been tempted to put down my pen in the middle of constructing an exciting scene," said Kit. "Just now I was wading through a history tome, trying to discover how often Anne, when she became Queen, was in direct contact with her half-brother, the Pretender to the throne. My belief is that one way and another she saw a good deal of him, but there's little to substantiate it. She was a pathetic creature, but a weathercock for weakness, influenced for and against him by first one person and then another."

"It must be wonderfully interesting to revive history and to put one's own interpretation on why historical characters acted as they did."

"So many of them were puppets, especially the women. Natural enough—they wanted to please the men they loved. That's a woman's nature."

"It's no more than a ready-made opinion. Women, whatever you may think, are not all alike."

"I agree, but there are basic characteristics."

"We have been conditioned through centuries of subservience to wish to please and to make the most of our persuasive powers."

"Exactly. Why are you in such revolt against it?"

"I am generally in revolt against unfairness. So are you, Kit, otherwise you would not have felt such indignation on your mother's behalf."

"Occasionally I wondered if that was not misplaced. Lately I have had the opportunity to study her. Few of us are helpless victims of fate. Our mamma had great influence with Lady Thora, who would not have refused her had she wished to have both her children with her. That was an alternative to leaving me with my father's brother."

"It's disappointing to find that you can be unjust and unappreciative. She had made a bargain with him she was sure was for your benefit, and in any case she could not go back on her word. Why do you look so skeptical?"

"I shall only affront you if I say that women of such rigid principle do not exist. If they have been conditioned through the years to charm, they have also been conditioned to scorn keeping a promise."

"It amuses you to affront me." Arabel laughed unwillingly.

"I suppose it does. It's a shame, but you look so really enchanting when you are angry. Green fire from your eyes, and a flush tinting that magnolia skin."

"Good heavens! One might think I was beautiful. As a child I was described as 'pasty.' At Seacrest they told me my eyes were peculiar, tilted at the corners or something. A mistress who did not like me once told me they made me look sly. But dear me, how easily I am drawn into talking about myself. I can't blame you if you despise me for my vanity."

"I wouldn't give a fig for a woman without vanity," Kit retorted, "and, far from despising you, I think you a darling, a generous darling. You would genuinely have preferred it had Mother inherited Lady Thora's estate, and you have made it plain that when you are in a position to do so you will provide liberally for her. As head of the family that should be my privilege, but although I can pay my own way, I can't do much for her until I have fully established myself as a writer."

"Of course you can't, and I'm thankful you don't

need to worry about Ursula. Do novels bring in a great deal of money?"

"It all depends if they appeal to the general public. My publishers think that mine will be popular. I do write with zest and enjoyment, and that does generally get through to the reader, I imagine."

"How exciting it will be to see your first book when it is published. It will be a big moment in Ursula's life. What is its title?"

"I have called it *The Heritage,* which serves a dual purpose, as it is the name of the hero's family home and also refers to his pride in being an Englishman, though England then was not what it is today, and life was certainly not rated as highly. Death was the penalty for even minor offences. But you probably know as much about the conditions then as I do, since until recently you believed it was your mission to teach the young."

"My necessity. I'm not a learned person, Kit, as I told you before, but please don't say again that that is no disadvantage."

He laughed. Affection and pleasure in her were to be read in his eyes. Arabel slightly shifted the angle of her parasol, shielding her face from him.

"Are you an adept at flirtation, Bel?"

The parasol was lowered and closed, and she said, "I should not be surprised to discover that you are, but it's ridiculous to flirt with me, your sister."

"I find it difficult to realize that I have a sister."

"Well, I dare say, we have seen so little of each other, but you will become accustomed to it."

"I wonder. It's good of you to let me stay here for a while and to go to so much trouble about a study for me."

"Nonsense! Troy Court should be a home for all of us."

"Only until you marry, Bel. By that time I hope I shall be in a position to give Mother a home with me."

"I do get so tired of this constant talk about my marriage, as though it is inevitable. Besides, Ursula may yet be the mistress of Troy Court."

"What in the world do you mean by that?"

Arabel hesitated. In truth she scarcely knew what had prompted the words, save that a poignant sadness, a wistfulness, had suddenly taken possession of her, deepening her voice, making her lips tremble and her eyes fill with tears. She said, "If I die, everything I have is hers, and sometimes I think . . ."

"You think—what?" Kit came to an abrupt standstill, and as abruptly he caught her hand, forcing her to face him.

"Oh nothing—really nothing—just the melancholy, saddening things one does think occasionally, for no reason at all. It's true what I say, though when Mr. Brecknell spoke of the possibility, Ursula was extremely upset and refused to listen to him. If I die before I come of age, all that Lady Thora left me reverts to Ursula. Of course there's no reason why I *should* die, except that since leaving Seacrest, I don't feel as well as I did there. I sleep badly, and I have horrid dreams in which I seem to be looking down on myself—a dead girl lying on the bed and I . . . I am saying good-bye to her. It means nothing, Kit. I'm not such a fool as to suppose it does. These last weeks have been distressing—too exciting— and then, as you know, I was ill with a chill and some fever. Perhaps I do have a slight rise in temperature now and again after dusk. Don't look so concerned, please."

"How do you expect me to look?" he asked with a roughness in his voice.

"Oh well—amused perhaps, tolerant of female foolish fancies. I assure you . . ." Arabel broke off, for a footman holding a silver salver was hastening to them across the grass.

She was relieved that Kit had dropped her hand, and that it must appear as though they were only in casual talk. She moved leisurely toward the hurrying man, listened with composure as he told her that visitors had arrived who, not content with leaving cards, had expressed a keen desire to see Miss Gibson if she was at home. The footman had thought it possible she was in the garden. Arabel took the small cards from the salver.

"A Mr. and Mrs. Digby," she told Kit, "and yes . . . oh joy, this card is Charlotte's. She has arrived sooner than I expected."

# CHAPTER 5

"It's like a wonderful fairy story," Charlotte said. "I thought so when I had your letter telling me about it, but now when I see this beautiful place, I wonder that you can be so calm over it all."

"I don't always feel calm inside myself," Arabel said.

The two girls were sitting in the small room that Mrs. Gibson called Arabel's boudoir, though probably it had been intended as a dressing room since there was a communicating door between it and the Chinese room. It was prettily furnished in a style for a pampered young woman, with a cream carpet and chairs upholstered in a flowered chintz. On the walls there were framed watercolors that Lady Thora had painted in her youth and that depicted various parts of the grounds—a bluebell glade in the woods, the rose garden, the yew garden. In each picture there was a background glimpse of Troy Court. Arabel, welcoming privacy, spent a good deal of her time in this room, which Charlotte thought pretty but ordinary in comparison with the Oriental grandeur of the bedroom.

"You always said you loved this place, Arabel, but it does seem extraordinary that just because you said you did as a child, Lady Thora should have left everything to you."

"It does indeed, but it's really only Ursula who has hit on such an explanation. She thinks it was a link between Lady Thora and me, and that as she felt the same she decided it should pass to one who would treasure it, though there's nothing in her will to indicate this, no indication that I must live at Troy Court and never sell it. I sometimes wish Ursula had been less honest, and pretended that she cared more for Troy Court—then, probably it would have been left to her. But she thought it far too large for one invalidish woman who, in any case, spent so little time here, and she often, she says now, urged Lady Thora to let it and to take a small place in or near London, which Ursula loves. One sees her point, of course. Money was poured out on the upkeep of the estate, and there were more servants than could be usefully employed. Although every room in the house was kept in order, it's ages since more than one wing has been in use—a terrible waste that has already started to worry me."

"But aren't you glad it has been bequeathed to you?" asked Charlotte wonderingly.

"Oh yes, of course, but I seem to have developed a conscience."

"What about?"

"There are so many people without proper homes— poor, aging, living in one room—people who have no ease or beauty in their lives. I sometimes wonder this did not occur to Lady Thora, but of course she was ill for so many years, and her chief preoccupation was trying to find a cure. I think as I grew up I should, if I had been much with her, have tried to rouse her, tried to give her something more than herself to brood over. She needed youth in her life, though she would have found Kit more stimulating than I am. Ursula says she had such admiration for creative writers."

"How handsome your brother is, Arabel, and in an unusual kind of way. Nicholas, my cousin, said after our first visit that you were the best-looking trio he had ever seen, though *you* don't in the least resemble either your mother or your brother."

"As to that, Kit is only my half-brother, and Ursula says that I am like my father. I do wish she had a photograph of him, but on her travels she lost the only one she possessed."

"What a pity," said Charlotte, not particularly interested. She sighed with satisfaction. "Isn't it wonderful to be together again like this, and it's such good luck that Cousin William has bought Green Lawns. They say they'd like me to stay for a few weeks, and Father and Mother won't mind, because they have to visit some old friends in Scotland and I've said all along that I don't want to go. Now it's as though we are still at Seacrest."

To see Charlotte again was even more pleasant than Arabel had anticipated. The tall, fair girl was sprawled out inelegantly in a big chair, her eyes resting with a doting expression upon Arabel, who said laughing, "If I were at Seacrest I should rebuke you for lolling."

"We're friends now, without the pupil-teacher barrier. Not that I don't wish you could be my governess, for, although I've told Mother I simply can't return to Seacrest as it would be unbearable without you, she says it's impossible for my education to come to an end when I'm only sixteen. A governess will have to be found for me, and I expect she'll be terrible."

"Would your parents consent to your living here at Troy Court, if you had visiting masters? I am not qualified to teach advanced subjects."

"Live here!" Charlotte altered her position and sat bolt upright. "Would it be possible?"

"For me, yes, but of course it depends upon your people." Arabel proceeded to outline the plan that for the last few days had been germinating in her mind.

"You're a witch, Arabel, you really are! I'm positive I can get the parents to agree. It's nearer than Seacrest when they want to visit me, and, as Cousins William and Grace live so near, they'd be all the better pleased. Mother is godmother to Nicholas. I'm not particularly wanted at home—at sixteen—for they do love to travel.

When I come out in another couple of years it will be different, for then I can go about with them, but until then a governess at home would mean they were tied down. I can't imagine anything that would make me happier. But what will your mother say? I know Troy Court is yours, but I expect you'd consult her about having a permanent guest."

"My mother will make no objection. Why should she?"

"But if this works out, my parents will expect to—to . . . what I mean is they wouldn't allow me to accept so much hospitality from anyone."

"Oh dear! That's a snag. Ursula would certainly balk at a paying guest, and if you did live here for a year or so, though I expect you'd want to go home on a visit from time to time, it would be as much to my advantage as yours. Knowing scarcely anyone in the neighborhood, I am really in need of companionship."

"And we always got on so marvelously well together. I'm sure we can work it out. Why shouldn't you come home with me for holidays, or stay in London with us, as we often do stay? That would sort of make it equal."

"It would be equal without that." But Arabel reflected that if Kit were at Troy Court her mother would have no objection to her visiting friends.

"As for not knowing people," Charlotte went on, "you very soon will. There are not only my Digby cousins but also the Wentworths. Father and Mother are friendly with them. They're great fun, always having houseparties and giving balls. You'll probably be the local belle, for sometimes you look more than pretty— quite beautiful."

Arabel laughed. "At Seacrest I was considered quite ordinary."

"You had to be, otherwise you wouldn't have been a suitable pupil teacher, let alone a junior mistress. Any girl can make herself plain if she intends to, and you wore such dowdy dresses and pinned back your hair so that nobody guessed how lovely it was. I thought you beautiful, of course, but all the same it gave me a shock when you glided into the drawing-room to meet us all, your skirts making that soft, frothing sound, and your hair piled up on high, and your long neck rising out of a mesh of lace like—like a swan."

At this Arabel burst out laughing, and Charlotte bounded from her chair and hugged her. "I always adored you, but more so than ever now for thinking of such a delightful plan."

"If it does come about, Charlotte, I hope with all my heart you will be happy here. I don't see why not. Kit is very good-natured and Ursula is kind to everyone."

"She certainly looks very kind," said Charlotte, but she had her mental reservations. She had always been decisive in her likes and dislikes, and although struck with Ursula Gibson's good looks and admitting that her voice and manner were benevolent, she was not drawn to her. Was she jealous of Arabel's mother? This thought crossed Charlotte's mind, but it seemed impossible, since the affection Arabel gave her was very different from that which she gave to Ursula. Many of Lady Thora's visitors had spoken approvingly of her housekeeper's warmth and consideration and desire to please, but Charlotte was not conscious of warmth. She suspected that Ursula would not want her to stay indefinitely at Troy Court, and she did not wonder that Arabel was lonely. To Charlotte's sharp young eyes there seemed to be little affinity between them, though Mrs. Gibson's devotion to Kit was evident. She seemed kind on the surface, but it would not surprise Charlotte to find that in truth she was anything but kind.

The Digbys at Green Lawns gave a small dinner party to which Ursula, Kit, and Arabel were invited. Quite informal, wrote Mrs. Digby in her short letter, designedly so, as they were in mourning. The only other guests would be the Wentworths from Tower House.

For Arabel it was an enjoyable occasion. The Digbys were an agreeable middle-aged couple, though Mr. Digby, who was small and hirsute, had none of the distinction the uninitiated connected with a Harley Street specialist. Charlotte was radiant. During the evening she told Arabel that she had written to her mother and had that day received her reply. Lady Frewin would be pleased for her to continue her studies under Arabel's supervision and wrote that all the difficulties connected with it could no doubt be satisfactorily adjusted. She would consult Charlotte's father and would then write to Arabel.

"But Father always does what Mother wants, so it's as good as settled," Charlotte said jubilantly. "What tremendous fun it will be."

Nicholas Digby also spoke of the proposed plan. He was a stockily built young man, and his blunt features were the kind of features one would expect to see on a bronzed face, but Nicholas's face was tallow pale and indicated recent illness, and his eyes, which were almost disconcertingly intelligent, looked slightly sunken. None of this was surprising, for the attack of typhoid fever had been severe. Nicholas had been taking things quietly, and even this small dinner party might be too much for him, but it had been arranged that if he felt tired he would slip away quietly. Although the numbers at the dinner table were uneven, this was of no consequence as they sat around an oval table. Arabel had Nicholas on one side of her, Tony Wentworth on the other. Nicholas's father was paying a more than ordinarily courteous attention to Ursula, or so Arabel thought. Tactlessly tactful was the phrase that occurred to her. Ursula was unaccustomed to being a guest at dinner parties, and wasn't Mr. Digby making it rather obvious that he recognized this fact? Although his intentions were excellent, Arabel's tinge of annoyance was sharp.

Cosette Wentworth, extremely elegant, with bronze

hair, a sharp-featured, piquant face, and a slight, rather attractive Boston accent, was describing a recently attended garden party at which some of the ex-Emperor Louis Napoleon's relations had been present. A memory stirred in Arabel's consciousness and was dredged up to the surface. A slight hiatus in the conversation gave her her opportunity. She leaned forward, dodged the centerpiece of tall, wired roses, and said, "Ursula, quite a few years ago now you met the Emperor Louis Napoleon in Paris. I was at school, but you wrote to me about it, telling me how pleased the Emperor was that Lady Thora and you were his guests. It was a very grand affair, wasn't it?"

"Too grand," said Ursula equably. "English visitors were very popular just then, for Queen Victoria had made the most tremendous impression upon Parisians, and the Empress Eugénie talked of her constantly. Lady Thora was asked so many questions about the Royal Family that she became quite exhausted, speechless, and would have been in even worse state, I dare say, but that I was with her and could supply details generally known, but which *she* never could remember . . . the exact ages of the royal children and so on. The Empress looked exquisite, and she was so gracious. She insisted on giving me what she called a trivial souvenir— this brooch which I often wear."

The brooch of pearls and sapphires fastening the lace on the bosom of Ursula's gown was duly admired. Arabel sat back in her chair well content. She had made her point. If Ursula could be the honored guest of an Emperor and Empress, even though they were now dethroned, there was no excuse for patronage by ordinary commoners.

"That was well done," murmured Nicholas beneath the hum of conversation.

Arabel glanced at him. His eyes were glinting with amusement; a smile hovered. His mouth, Arabel noticed, was his best feature, firm yet sensitive, with clean-shaven

lips. She supposed he was thirty-three or thirty-four,
though he sometimes looked older. After a moment she
returned his smile and said, also in a low tone, "If only
they don't remember that the Empress Eugénie has often
been called a parvenue."

"All the Napoleon clan have been called that at different times, but it doesn't detract from their dazzling
quality. But why do you feel called upon to fight your
mother's battle? I should say there were few more
capable of holding their own."

"*Would* you?" This was not a matter she had considered. "But she's as gentle in her way as Lady Thora
was—and vulnerable too, which Lady Thora hadn't any
need to be. Mrs. Wentworth was so loftily ignoring her,
but my mother will put up with that without rancor,
rather than see me isolated and lonely."

"You won't be, and my impression of your mother is
that she cares very little about local attitudes. Why
should she? She's a cosmopolitan at heart."

"Yes, perhaps she is. She has traveled so much, and
although I didn't know it until lately, Troy Court and
the country bore her."

"If the place were hers," said Nicholas, "she would
have it up for sale in no time; a smart little London
bandbox—Mayfair for choice—would suit her better.
I sympathize, for I am also addicted to London, which
is fortunate, as I shall be spending most of my life
there."

"In Harley Street. As a doctor—a specialist?"

"Eventually, but being a doctor I know it will be
months before I am fit. Not to make a start exactly. I
have been in partnership with my father for the past
eight years, but after such a long lapse it will be a hard
thing to pick up again."

Arabel said sympathetically, "It's terribly unfortunate
that you have been so ill."

"It depends which way you look at it. You could say
I am extremely fortunate to be this side of Jordan and

on the mend. Moreover, so far as I can judge I shall not be left with any side effects. I have had all the medical tests lately and I know they are sound. Oh, good lord! I've been meandering on about myself for at least ten minutes, though you are partly to blame for putting up such a good show of concern and interest."

"It isn't only a show. I do feel concern and interest. Apart from you personally, your work is of such importance. Charlotte, I suppose, doesn't know a great deal about it, but she was telling me how impressed her parents were with your father's methods. She said he had in some cases not only prolonged the lives of patients with heart troubles, but also had cured them. What I mean is, they seem to be as good as new."

Nicholas glanced smilingly across the table at Charlotte, who, judging from the laughter evoked, was holding an amusing conversation with Kit and Cosette Wentworth. "I should scarcely have thought my vivacious cousin capable of discussing anything serious," he said indulgently.

"You underrate her, Mr. Digby. She's a clever girl, though I suppose you will say, as most gentlemen say, that that is more of a misfortune than an asset—no qualification for marriage, which should be a girl's supreme aspiration."

"Not at all. I can think of few fates worse for a man than to possess a brainless life partner, though as the world is at present, marriage does seem to give a woman more outlet than other avocations."

"Not all women think so—there's Florence Nightingale, for instance, and Miss Burdett-Coutts."

"Pioneers!"

"Well, isn't your father a pioneer, and won't you be?"

"*Touché!*" Nicholas regarded her with a greater interest. "Tell me, have you any unorthodox aspirations?"

"Vague ones. I've only recently acquired any power —if being in possession of a house and estate such as Troy Court, and the money that goes with it, signifies power—but I do think it's unlikely I shall find any real satisfaction in a purely social life. I would like to do some good in the world, not only just to marry and to have a husband and a family. Troy Court is so beautiful and so much too large for one family. I should grieve to give it up or not to live there, but one large wing is sufficient for a family, and Troy Court has three wings. I wish sometimes that I could share it. Two of the wings have been unused for nearly a generation—lovely large rooms with splendid views. As yet I have no power, but when I am of age . . ."

"Have you some special plan in mind?" Nicholas asked.

"It is all so clouded at present, but I did think it might be possible to have people to stay who are in need of rest and freedom from care, while getting over serious illnesses, people who can't afford to pay fees." Arabel dropped her voice to an even lower note. "I don't know what I can do—as yet, and my mother is not sympathetic to such ideas. Lady Thora thought it her duty to keep Troy Court exactly as her ancestors had kept it—a family possession to be preserved in perfection. It seems odd that as she felt that way she should have left it to me with no conditions attached. After all, she *did* have distant relations bearing her name, and I was nothing to her but her housekeeper's daughter. She was fond of me. She took an interest in me, paid for my education, but even so . . ."

Arabel broke off with a faintly troubled expression, and Nicholas said, "You have plenty of time in which to think over matters, but it is a noble aim, so don't let yourself be discouraged. As I understand it, you can make no move for a year or more."

"Fourteen months it is now. If I die before then, everything passes to my mother. But she is upset to think there is even a bare possibility of that."

"Very natural. But should you, when you are somewhat older, be of the same mind, I hope you will let me know."

"Would you help me, Mr. Digby?"

"Assuredly, if it is in my power. Could you bring yourself to call me Nicholas? Less confusing, as I am at present living under my father's roof."

"Wouldn't *Mr*. Nicholas be more proper, as we have only known each other such a short time?"

"Not when one takes into consideration that you are my young second cousin's beloved friend, and also, she tells me, are likely to become her guide and mentor. Besides, does forming a friendship depend on length of time? I wouldn't say so—not in all circumstances. We have progressed in knowledge of each other within a few hours."

"I suppose there is something in that," Arabel allowed.

"There's a great deal in it, Arabel, and I'm bold enough to take your permission for granted."

The reserve that Arabel acquired at Seacrest College and that had won Miss Norton's commendation broke suddenly, and a smile flashed. "I shall be delighted if you will call me Arabel and delighted if we can be friends."

His smile answered hers. "What a bore that we are not alone, with no watching eyes upon us, for then we could have sealed the pact with a fervent handclasp."

"You were quite taken up with young Mr. Digby," said Ursula. "Mr. Wentworth on your other side made several attempts to divert your attention, but without success."

"Did he? Mrs. Digby and he are old friends and they seemed to have plenty to say to each other. They hadn't met for some time, she said, as the Wentworths have been traveling abroad. I found Nicholas extremely interesting."

"That," said Kit, "was obvious. You have taken little time to get to a given-name basis."

The party had broken up at a fairly early hour. Ursula, on their return to Troy Court, had said that Arabel looked tired, but she did not feel tired. The conversation with Nicholas had stimulated her, had drawn her out of herself, banishing her habitual reserve. Now she sparkled at them. "Are you finding fault with me?" she inquired.

"Not really," Kit said. "You were the big attraction of the evening. She looked lovely, didn't she, Mother?" And then Ursula made a gesture of assent. "But I was curious—such animation, though in conversation with Digby I found it heavy going. Did you hit on some absorbing topic?"

"Well, yes, his work, chiefly, and his father's work. It's too bad he has been ill for so long. He is fretting to start again, but it will be a long time yet before he can. One day I'd like to take him all over Troy Court. I was telling him about the two wings that have been shut up for a generation."

"But not neglected," Mrs. Gibson said, jealous for her efficiency as a housekeeper. "There's not a room in the entire place that could not be used at an hour's notice."

"I know—it's wonderful. Structural repairs can take months and are costly I expect. I *was* outlining a kind of vague scheme."

Her mother uttered a dismayed exclamation. "Oh, Arabel, not that peculiar idea you once began to discuss with me! A crazy notion of turning Troy Court into a convalescent home."

"Only part of it. And is it really so crazy? I haven't thought of it as a convalescent home exactly, only of giving a few people who have been ill and are not well off a rest from time to time. Nicholas was interested and encouraging. He thought it would be very helpful to people who need help."

"Surely he can have little acquaintance with such people. A Harley Street specialist charges high fees that only rich patients can pay."

Kit interposed, "As to that, Digby Senior was a consultant at two London hospitals and must have come into contact with many who could not pay such fees."

"And," Arabel supplemented, "Nicholas says that many have great difficulty in finding the money and cannot even follow a specialist's advice. They have to go on working even though it threatens their lives."

Mrs. Gibson sighed pityingly. "Poor souls—one hears so many tragic stories, but even if you did receive a few ailing people here, it would be no more than a drop in the ocean."

"Isn't every drop important when it represents an individual and isn't it possible one might inspire others to do the same sort of thing?"

"I very much doubt it. Don Quixotes are rare. I wish you would put this foolish dream out of your mind. Charitable donations are all very well, and Lady Thora was most liberal in that way, but to turn Troy Court into a charitable institution is very different. The upkeep would swallow a large proportion of your income, and the place would be ruined. Imagine a host of strangers let loose in the grounds. Not only would privacy be violated, but the gardens would be ruined. There would have to be nurses as well, and possibly a resident doctor. You would soon find that your home belonged more to them than to yourself. Only a young and inexperienced girl could envisage such a scheme."

Arabel was astonished by her mother's unwonted heat. Kit was inclined to be amused. He said, "But it is all in the air as yet. Bel can do nothing for well over a year, and by then, probably, she will want something quite different. It should be enough for her, for the time being, to take the adoring Charlotte under her wing. I am in sympathy with that project, are not you, Mother?"

"I am not sure. If the girl obstinately refuses to return to Seacrest College, it would seem to be more natural for her to live at home or with her cousins at Green Lawns."

"But Bel is the attraction," said Kit, "and she has the experience to supervise Charlotte's studies, which Mrs. Digby has not; nor the time, since she has a home to run for her husband and son. It will be a diversion as well as an occupation for Bel, who has so much energy. Charlotte, who is a nice child, will draw both of you into her circle of friends here. It means acceptance in this class-conscious neighborhood, which, now that Bel is one of the chief landowners, is bound to be of importance to her."

"I agree there may be advantages," said Mrs. Gibson reluctantly, "and I should be sorry to see Arabel socially isolated, though for myself it is not of much importance. Charlotte Frewin can easily be accommodated here, but I hope it will not be misconstrued—that people will not think we benefit financially."

Arabel protested, "Of course they won't. Charlotte and I have already worked that out. There will be an exchange of visits. When her people are home, I shall often stay there with her. You wouldn't be lonely, Ursula, not with Kit here."

"But you have heard your brother say that he intends to live in London."

"Well, yes, for headquarters—but you like it here, don't you, Kit?"

"I do, indeed. It's a most glorious old place, and the library—for a private library—is second to none."

"Then when I am away, couldn't you stay here?"

"Very frequently, probably."

Mrs. Gibson observed her daughter with a slightly wintry smile. "You have a managing disposition, my dear, and as Kit says, a great deal of energy, if it can be called such. A more accurate description might be feverish excitement. I wish I could see you more placid and content, and then you would sleep soundly at nights without the aid of my soothing tisanes."

"Even taking them I don't sleep well," Arabel said, wondering if she was indeed abnormally overwrought as her mother sometimes hinted. It was true that within her there was a restlessness, a disturbance that she had never known while at Seacrest College. There she had been serene, if not actually happy.

"Your insomnia would be much worse if you did not take this nightly tisane," Mrs. Gibson said, and Arabel did not contradict her. She might be right, though she was rather amused by her mother's faith in ancient herbal remedies. They were a hobby with her, thought Arabel. She spent a considerable time in the stillroom, brewing and distilling and experimenting, improving on the recipes in the old book she had discovered, and which she kept under lock and key, refusing to allow even Arabel to examine it. Arabel suspected that the ingredients of the homemade medicines were so simple and innocuous that her mother feared derision. If they wrought cures, prevented colds, soothed coughs, induced sleep, this was partly because Ursula's faith communicated itself to those who swallowed her draughts, which were generally pleasant, hot and spiced and sugared.

Now glancing at the clock, Mrs. Gibson remarked that it was much later than they usually retired. Kit might, as he usually did, work until past midnight, writing in the library or his now adequately furnished study, but Arabel should be in bed.

"Do forgo that hot bath for once, dear," she urged, "and I will bring you your tisane, and see you tucked up comfortably before I go to bed myself. I worry about you. I am convinced you are still losing weight, and your appetite is so capricious, though Cook follows all instructions and does her best to tempt you."

"There's no need to worry. I eat more than I ever

did at Seacrest." But Arabel was touched by her mother's concern, and gathering up her evening cloak and bag, she moved toward the door that Kit held open for her.

# CHAPTER 6

That night, Arabel tossed restlessly for some time before she fell asleep, longing for the sweet oblivion that had once been a commonplace, something to accept as a matter of course. It was a hot, airless night, and there was little benefit to be derived from the wide-open windows.

The darkness was welcome since it was impossible for the mind to dwell on the fantastic Chinese landscape, though in the normal way this had ceased to trouble her, and she no longer wished to change her room; she had become accustomed to exotic luxury, and in contrast Lady Thora's suite was simple. She had slept in a narrow white bed without hangings and had gathered around her treasures of her childhood and girlhood. The furniture was of ivory-painted wood with pale pink handles on the doors of chests and wardrobe. These matched the pink roses on the carpet. When Arabel had entered this room as a child and a young girl, Lady Thora having expressed the wish to see her, she had much admired the color scheme, but now it seemed insipid. Yet had she been given a room at Seacrest College that was only half as attractive, she would have been enchanted.

I've changed so much even in a few weeks, thought Arabel with perplexity.

She had been docile but now was obstinate. If she

did not precisely defy her mother, she at least made it plain that she was preparing for the day when she would be her own mistress, and even now she was asserting independence. Ursula, she knew, though she had given way over the plan concerning Charlotte, was loath to have the girl at Troy Court for any length of time, which was natural, Arabel admitted with some remorse, since this was her first opportunity of having both her children under the same roof with her. But in wishing to include Charlotte permanently in their circle Arabel was ensuring congenial occupation for herself, and she would probably divert and amuse Kit. Surely when he was not working on his book he must often be slightly bored. Ordinarily they saw few people, and the continual companionship of a mother and sister could not be exciting.

Thinking thus, a deeply submerged sense of guilt struggled to the surface, for, though she was not exciting to Kit, she was forced to admit that he was disturbingly so to her. He, she guessed, charmed women without being aware of it. It meant nothing to him when he paid her compliments, when, bidding her goodnight, he lightly kissed her cheek. Why should it, indeed, and why should it be so troubling to her, leaving her pulses throbbing and her heart thudding? Was she happy or unhappy? She could not be sure, for there was a strange sweetness in the sense of bruised sorrow that so often swept over her.

They were not often alone together, but when her mother was out, it did seem to Arabel that Kit deliberately sought for her and found it pleasant to be in her company. He *was* fond of her, Arabel supposed. He certainly had been when she was a child, and more than once he had said how much he regretted that they had seen nothing of each other for years. It must seem natural to him to join her when he saw her walking in the garden, generally to talk to her about the book he was writing. Arabel would have found these conversations enjoyable even had he meant nothing to her, for, when discussing the actions of his characters, he had the knack of bringing them vividly to life. But Charlotte, who, although so young, was intelligent and loved history, would be an even better audience, thought Arabel determinedly.

Behind her closed eyes, she felt the pricking of tears. She had not supposed that such mental turmoil was possible. She had practiced self-discipline from childhood, and it was a cruel thing that it should now desert her. Fond though I am of Charlotte, she thought, I have always been inclined to use her, and I am planning to use her now. But it's not as though it will do her any harm.

Presently the dreaminess she had longed for began to steal over her, but it did not take entire possession of her. Half of her mind seemed to be still awake. The night was too hot to be endurable, and, although she was covered only by the sheet and a thin blanket, she threw them aside. Now she was sitting on the side of the bed and had the sensation of gasping for air; yet she had no consciousness of standing on her feet, of gazing first at the open window and then at the closed door. Finally she walked across to the door and turned the handle.


In the library, which Kit still preferred to the study on the first floor, especially when he worked late at night, he scribbled the lines that brought him to the end of a chapter. He wasn't altogether satisfied with it, but then when was he ever satisfied? The next day when he read it over again, there would be copious revisions. Tonight he was too tired, and he pushed back his chair from the desk, yawned hugely and stretched out his arms. It was past two o'clock and more than time for him to seek his bed.

At this hour he was so accustomed to the complete

silence of the old house, that at first, when he heard or thought he heard a sound without, he paid no attention to it. It was a faint sound which he would not have heard at all, except that for the sake of coolness, the door as well as the window was half-open. A moment later, he distinctly heard a rustle and a soft sigh, and he was then conscious of a chilly, prickling sensation at the nape of his neck. He had been told about the ghost of the little Chinese bride, though his mother scoffed and said that so far as she knew nobody had ever seen it, and it was a definite effort to get to the door and throw it wide open. From there he had a clear view of the wide parquet stairs which led to the first floor. Down them glided a figure in white.

For a split second, awe held him, and then the spell broke. This was no apparition, but Arabel, looking more beautiful than he had ever seen her look, though utterly unfamiliar in her flowing night robe, her feet bare and her dark hair loose on her shoulders. He spoke her name, but she did not answer, nor turn her head toward him. She stared straight ahead of her with unseeing eyes, swayed slightly, and yet did not clutch at the banister rail.

Sudden understanding struck upon Kit. She was walking in her sleep, and although her eyes were wide open they were blind eyes. A bare foot slid on the highly polished parquet, and she lurched forward; but in that heart-stopping moment Kit sprang to receive in his arms the slight, fragile burden of a flimsily clad body. As he did so, he must, he realized, have cried out her name again, for his mother's door, which was nearest to the head of the stairs, opened, and she spoke, her voice staccato with alarm and demanding an explanation.

Kit gave none. He was too occupied with Arabel, who clung to him. She was awake now, but, as was evident to him, was so bewildered that she did not *know* she was awake. An arm went up to encircle his neck, and with a tranced half-smile she drew his face down to hers, inviting the kiss which, without forethought or hesitation, Kit bestowed. The sweet sense of union was only momentary, for submissive yielding was followed by a shuddering sigh and a spasmodic trembling.

Carrying her into the library, Kit said softly, "Don't be frightened . . . now you're awake and safe. . . ."

He lowered her to the sofa to find his mother at his side. She had flung on a wrap and had thrust her feet into soft slippers.

"What happened?" she asked tersely.

"Sleepwalking. I had just finished work when I heard her on the stairs. She slipped and would have fallen headlong, except that I caught her. She half-awoke as she was falling, and it must have given her a shock— otherwise no harm has come to her."

"Even now she's not fully awake," said Ursula. She bent over Arabel and gently prized open the fingers that still clutched at Kit's coat.

"Brandy, do you think?" he asked.

His mother shook her head negatively. There were beads of sweat on Arabel's brow, though she shivered again, and Kit took the sofa rug and wrapped it about her.

"Oh don't! I'm so hot," she protested and struggled into a sitting position. "I remember feeling suffocated before I fell asleep."

Even as she spoke, she was yawning, her heavy eyes closing. Mrs. Gibson said, "Probably she'll remember nothing of this in the morning. Take hold of one of her arms, Kit, and I will take the other, and then we can get her up the stairs to her room."

Kit, who was visibly shaken, said doubtfully, "But is it safe to leave her?"

"Yes, I think so. It's improbable she will walk in her sleep again, not twice on the same night, but as a precaution I'll bolt the window in her room, and I could lock the door on the outside and open it early in the morning. Tomorrow we can think of better safety devices, but I've heard it said that somnambulists rarely come to any harm; they unconsciously protect themselves."

"Bel didn't. She could have been killed. I told you she slipped on the stairs."

"But not necessarily to fall down the length of them. Only a few steps, probably."

Kit said no more. His mother might be right. Between them, Arabel was half-led, half-carried up the stairs and laid on her bed. Kit went down to the library to put away his papers. He stood for a while in thought, remembering the silken brush of Arabel's curling hair against his cheek, the softness of her body through the thin night robe. Most vivid memory of all was the pressure of her mouth on his. It was ridiculous, he thought, to attach any importance to an incident that tomorrow Arabel would not remember. All the same, he knew he would never forget it. Hitherto he had not analysed his emotional reaction to her, but now he was forced to it.

Certainly he had taken great pleasure in her, had been delighted and surprised by her charming looks, her poise, her intelligence. Occasionally it had irritated him because he so seldom saw her alone. It did not strike him even now that over this his mother and Arabel had been silently and unknowingly in league. Arabel wishing to avoid him, and Mrs. Gibson possessively unwilling to share him even with her daughter.

Kit now admitted to himself that there had been moments when he had been agreeably stirred by Arabel's charm, but as this had often happened with young women whom he had found no difficulty in forgetting, this had not troubled him; nor had it grazed his consciousness that it was singular to experience such a stimulating of the nerves where his half-sister was concerned.

The thing was, he mused ruefully, that he couldn't regard Arabel as a sister, which after their long separation was not surprising. Besides, she was only a half-sister and had been more or less forgotten. His mother in her letters had rarely mentioned her, and Arabel herself had only occasionally written to him. A pity we're not cousins instead of half-brother and half-sister, thought Kit, even now scarcely realizing what had happened to him.

Footsteps in the hall, this time not at all ghostly, warned him that his mother had left Arabel. She stood in the doorway, and stacking his sheets of manuscript he glanced round with a stifled irritation. Mrs. Gibson had a tray in her hands. She said, "After such a shock, I dare say you will welcome a drink, and I collected some biscuits and cheese from the pantry."

There were two glasses, a decanter and a siphon on the tray. With the evident intention of staying for a while, Mrs. Gibson seated herself. She poured out a large whisky for Kit, a smaller one for herself, which she liberally diluted with soda water.

"You ought to be in bed," Kit said. "At this rate, it'll be dawn before we get any sleep."

"Very likely, but you can sleep as late as you wish, and so can I—now. Time was when I was up at seven without fail every morning. It's a luxury to be able to suit myself as to when I rise—not that dear Lady Thora would have complained; she always said I had far too little rest, but it was a routine hard to break. Besides, she might have needed me."

Seldom garrulous, Mrs. Gibson was garrulous now. Evidently she was still upset. The hand that held her glass trembled. Kit's irritation waned, and he said kindly, "I am sorry you woke up. I could have gotten Bel back to her room without much trouble."

"But you would have felt very uneasy about her. You might," and Ursula smiled bleakly, "have decided to sit up all night with her."

"Well, I don't know. It certainly scared me; for a moment I thought she was a ghost. Is Bel especially overwrought do you think? Perhaps Galbraith ought to have a look at her."

"Yes. I'll send a note round to him, though I'm puzzled as to how much to tell him. If Arabel remembers nothing, it might be unwise to enlighten her."

"Isn't a doctor the right person to decide that?"

"I suppose so, but . . . oh Kit, my dear, I'm worried. One doesn't want to reveal all one's private affairs, even to the family doctor."

Kit gazed at her puzzled. "My dear Mamma, one might think there was something disgraceful about the somnambulist incident. Surely to goodness you don't imagine Bel was pretending?"

"Good heavens, no! What an idea! But for years I have been at peace about her, Kit. Such a quiet, sensible girl, such a good girl, anxious not to be an additional worry to me. I was convinced the danger had passed, that she could not be affected by it."

Kit set down his half-empty glass. "What in the world do you mean?"

"I'm not sure. It may be of less importance than I fear. I hope it is. Perhaps after all it's not necessary to tell you."

"It most certainly is necessary—now." Kit's face was unusually grim. "You have said too much, not to say everything that is in your mind."

"Oh dear!" Ursula Gibson's placidity had deserted her. She gulped down the contents of her glass, as though hoping thereby to find courage. "At least it is not on *your* father's side."

"*What* isn't?"

"The Heralds are all level-headed, stable people. I suppose the one unconventional, reckless thing your father ever did was to marry me, who was so much beneath him. I was truly devoted to him, and that he knew, but I did wonder sometimes that he, so prudent, had allowed himself to be carried away through love of me. Arabel's father was very, very different."

"In what way?"

"Every way. It fascinated me. He was laughing and gay, and to meet him you would think that nothing in the world worried him. It was only when you really got to know him that you discovered otherwise. When he wasn't exhilarated it was just the opposite; then he was in the depths of black depression, frighteningly so. There seemed no real reason for either extreme. I never understood, or at least not until just before his last voyage. He hated to leave me, and it would be for months. He said sometimes he was haunted because of his family history. His mother had died in an asylum, raving mad, and he was, he said, very like her."

"In looks, did he mean?" Kit asked.

"In every way. She also had her moods. He, Bernard, could remember her. A pretty creature, he said she was; dark and slim and full of melancholy one minute and joy the next. He hadn't seen her since he was a boy. She was shut away for years before she died, and his father died of the grief of it. I reproached Bernard when he told me about her. I said I had had the right to know before I married him. And that was true enough, though I tried to comfort him and wanted him to forgive me, as I forgave him, I couldn't rouse him out of his misery. He left for his ship without a kind word for me, and I went to Lady Thora as had been arranged. Soon afterward I found I was going to have a child. I wrote to Bernard, a letter addressed to his next port of call, to tell him so, but whether or not he received that letter I've never known, nor if it had anything to do with what happened, for midway through that voyage he threw himself overboard. It was deliberate—no accident. He came up on top deck, spick-and-span in his best uniform, so I was told, and waved his hand to those of the crew who were within sight of him, and then—over he went! They tried to rescue him, of course, but it was no good—there was a heavy sea and sharks about in those waters. . . ."

Ursula shuddered and hid her face in her hands. Aghast and compassionate, Kit went to her, sat down beside her, put his arm round her. "What a ghastly thing! Poor chap and poor you! But surely you haven't been blaming yourself all these years?"

"Sometimes I have. Sometimes I've thought that what I said to him, being so shocked, was only what any wife would have said, for he *should* have told me, Kit, though I dare say I would have married him all the same. He was so handsome, with such an infectious smile and laugh, and he was madly in love with me. . . . Madly! Oh, how easily one uses that dreadful word. If I had been prepared I would have been kinder when he told me, but he caught me unaware. You can imagine something of my despair when I heard he was dead."

"It must have been terrible . . . the more so, I suppose, because of the expected baby."

"Yes. I didn't want her. I was afraid. I think but for Lady Thora I should have gone out of my mind. But I had her to look after."

"She wasn't ill then, was she? Not all those years ago?"

For an instant Mrs. Gibson looked bewildered. She passed her hand across her eyes and said, "I get confused. I shouldn't have taken that whisky. Spirits never did agree with me. No, she wasn't ill, the attack of rheumatic fever came later, but she was very unhappy over her father's death through a heart attack. As sudden as Bernard's death, though not nearly so dreadful. We—we helped each other through a great deal, and she was sure that travel, change of scene, was the best thing. We were abroad for months, and Arabel was born in Switzerland. From the first, Lady Thora took a great interest in her. Once she was here, I loved her, for that is nature's way, but I was in dread that she might inherit her father's malady. Gradually that fear died. Lady Thora insisted on paying for Arabel's education and no expense spared. She did well at Seacrest College;

her reports were excellent. It was such a relief to know she was considered a credit, a good influence; and then she was offered a position as pupil teacher and would have been one of the residential mistresses when she was older. Lady Thora had wanted to have Arabel here as a young companion, but I wouldn't agree. There was no future in such a position, or so I thought. I wasn't in Lady Thora's confidence about the inheritance she secretly planned. Kit, it is that that has so changed Arabel I fear. It has brought to the surface all that might have lain latent forever, if she had not suffered this dizzy change."

"You mean that a quiet, disciplined life, a life resembling a nun's, suited her?"

"It was safe for her. This bequest has upset Arabel's equilibrium. She has changed greatly, and I have watched with dread. She, who until this happened was so serene, so sensible, has become feverish, excitable, and is making the most foolish plans for the future. She has lost weight, eats little, sleeps badly—she is influenced by every passing mood. Oh Kit, it's her father all over again."

Ursula covered her face with her hands and was shaken by a dry sob. Kit's expression was grave, but he said reasonably, "Oh, come now, that's taking a far too gloomy view. Any girl might well become overexcited when her life changed so drastically. Besides, you told me Bel had been ill. . . ."

"Nothing serious, only a feverish chill. I was so concerned over her mental state that I made the most of it, hoping to disguise her—her strangeness. But this evening, surely this wild scheme to turn Troy Court into some sort of invalid's home convinces you of her—her derangement."

"Well, I can't say it does. It's no more than an altruistic enthusiasm that will probably come to nothing. Even if it did, the house, as she truly says, is enormous.

Bel is warm-hearted, sympathetic, and she was fired I dare say by the talk she had with Nicholas Digby."

"She had something of the sort in her mind before then. It's absurd—a young girl with no experience. How could she hope to make a success of such a project?"

"She could not immediately, but she had no thought of taking impulsive action, which in any case is out of her power while she is still underage."

"But you saw how excited she was over it, and the sleepwalking was a direct result. It's not only the hatching of a scheme, of which, as you say, she may soon tire—there's this girl, Charlotte Frewin. Arabel is determined she shall live here for the next year, and as Sir John and Lady Frewin have agreed, it has gone too far to be nipped in the bud."

"But that, socially, may be an advantage. Also, having a young girl as a companion, being more or less responsible for her, will be good for Bel, I should think. A fresh interest and occupation."

Mrs. Gibson reluctantly assented. "Yes, well, it may not be too bad, though to me it seems most unnatural. At Arabel's age and with so much to make life desirable, she should be thinking of her own enjoyment. One fear I have is that Charlotte Frewin, who is evidently a sharp-witted girl, may soon realize that Arabel isn't—isn't normal. With such a dread hovering over us, there's danger in taking another person into our family circle."

"My dear, I think you may be exaggerating the danger. In any case you should feel better now that you have opened your heart to me. It's no longer your sole burden. You know I'll do anything I possibly can to help, and as I'm no longer in the dark, I can guard Bel—calm her and influence her, possibly."

"Yes, perhaps you can, and it *is* a great thing to have been able to tell you, though I expect I shall reproach myself for having put such a burden on your shoulders."

"They're broad enough to support it. Now don't worry any more. We are both dropping on our feet for want of sleep, and we can talk over this again, at leisure, when we both feel more clearheaded."

Ursula smiled gratefully and tenderly at her son. "If only you could stay here always. *Must* you live in London? It means so much to have you here."

Kit stifled a yawn. Longing for sleep, he was not prepared to discuss this or anything else at the moment. "Well, we shall see. There's no immediate hurry, but I can't trespass on Bel's hospitality indefinitely."

"Kit—how absurd! Your own sister. Besides, you have heard her say that Troy Court is as much my home as hers. Arabel is very fond of you and is only too pleased to have you here."

Which might, thought the perturbed Kit, be true in a sense unsuspected by his mother. Escorting her to her room, they paused outside the Chinese room. Ursula took a key from the pocket of her dressing gown and opened the door. A night-light was burning, and standing side by side they looked down on Arabel, who was now deeply and peacefully asleep, her hair spreading like a dark fan on the pillow and her hand beneath her cheek.

"Poor, poor child," murmured Mrs. Gibson, "but she is safe enough now and will sleep for hours. Better not to lock the door again. If she woke before I did and found herself a prisoner, she would be terrified."

She stooped to kiss Arabel's brow. Kit's heart ached for them both, and in a strange, dazed fashion for himself.

# CHAPTER 7

The next morning, Arabel, as her mother had expected, remembered nothing about her disturbed night, though there were dark smudges beneath her eyes and she owned to having a headache; for this reason she was easily persuaded to stay in bed until just before luncheon.

Nothing was said to her about sleepwalking, and Ursula was convinced that for the time being at least there was no necessity to consult Dr. Galbraith. Rather against his better judgment Kit agreed to this. It was natural, he thought, that his mother should be loath to tell anyone of the taint in her daughter's blood, especially as it was possible that it might remain forever dormant.

When Arabel appeared at luncheon looking much as usual and wearing a gown which was most becoming to her, black being relieved by a shoulder-wide collar of fine white needle-work lace, Kit's heart was heavy for her. He found it singularly difficult to carry on a natural conversation, and more than once Arabel glanced at him inquiringly.

The meal was barely over when Charlotte arrived, her usual bouncy, happy self. Nicholas, she said, was waiting for her at the end of the avenue in his new, high dogcart. He was driving himself. If she and Arabel squeezed together, there would be room for both of them beside him. Would she care to venture?

Arabel said she would be delighted, but her mother pursed her lips and remarked that as Mr. Digby was still only convalescent, it would seem to be too much exertion for him to drive a spirited bay, to which Charlotte replied that he wouldn't risk it unless he felt strong enough, and added unnecessarily that after all Nicholas was a doctor and therefore a fit judge of what he could do and what he could not. They did not intend to be out for long, but proposed to take Arabel back with them to have tea at Green Lawns. "Nicholas," said Charlotte, "has told me about your wish to open up part of Troy Court for sick people who need somewhere beautiful to stay where they can get well. He thinks it is the most wonderful, generous idea, and so do I. Are you truly serious, dearest Arabel?"

"Yes, truly serious, but I explained that I could do nothing about it for over a year," Arabel replied.

"But a year or so soon passes. Oh, Arabel, you were such a success last evening, everyone admired you, and Nicholas says he has never met a girl like you."

"There *is* no other girl like her," said Kit. "That's one reason why we have to take the greatest care of her. Bel, you'd be wiser to stay at home this afternoon and rest."

Puzzled by his concern, Arabel said, "But my headache has vanished, and its only people who are elderly or really ill who insist on resting in the afternoon."

"Nonetheless," put in Ursula, "Kit is right. You have not been well lately and have had far too much excitement."

Arabel glanced down from one perturbed face to the other, shrugged and decided that as they were both genuinely distressed about her, it would be unkind to insist on having her own way. "Very well, then," she acceded, "I will stay at home, but get Nicholas to bring you back here, Charlotte, when you have had your drive."

Charlotte was by no means pleased over this altera-tion, but at Seacrest College she had been accustomed to render obedience, and the habit still held. Without further argument she rejoined her cousin and drove off with him.

"Why does Mrs. Gibson treat Arabel as though she's an invalid?" she said discontentedly as they bowled along the country road. "She's always telling her she looks too flushed or too pale or tired or something. But there was never anything wrong with Arabel when she was at Seacrest, and all that has been wrong with her since she left is a chill, which was caused from getting wet in a thunderstorm. Do you think she looks delicate?"

Nicholas did not immediately give the reassuring answer that Charlotte expected as a matter of course. "Not exactly delicate," he said at last, "but she certainly seems overstrung or overwrought. I forget now what occurred to bring up the subject of health; we were certainly not discussing it. I believe she asked me if typhoid had left me with a tendency to insomnia, and when I said it had not, she remarked that I could be thankful for it, as few things were more trying than to be awake hour after hour in a silent house, knowing that everyone else was blissfully asleep. Mrs. Gibson may be slightly overmaternal, but that is excusable if she is worried about Arabel."

"She wasn't particularly maternal when Arabel was at Seacrest. She had to spend most of her holidays there, and I know Mrs. Gibson didn't write too often. It's only since she inherited Troy Court and such a lot of money that she's been treated with such an excess of care."

"And what do you deduce from that?" Nicholas asked, with an amused, sidelong glance at her.

"I don't know exactly. Mrs. Gibson is dependent on

Arabel now, I imagine. Her brother is nice, amusing and clever, and from what Arabel has told me it wasn't his fault they saw so little of each other for years. I like him, but I *don't* like Mrs. Gibson. It's a Doctor Fell thing—I've no reason for it."

"If you don't like her, Charlotte, will it really be a good thing for you to be a permanent guest there?"

"Yes. I think it will." Her voice was decisive and oddly mature. "I have—well, it's a kind of intuition. Something seems to tell me that Arabel needs me. I believe that was why she suggested supervising my studies, though I'm sure she doesn't realize it. She wants me there as a friend, not as a sort of glorified pupil."

"I dare say she does. Someone lighthearted and only a few years younger than herself. Her brother is not likely to be a permanency, is he?"

"No. Arabel said that in the Autumn he would be living in London, near the British Museum, necessary to him for research on his book."

After a slight pause, Nicholas said, "If you are not happy at Troy Court, you can always live at Green Lawns. Father and Mother would be delighted to have you, though they *do* think you should have gone back to Seacrest for a further year, and that it was a mistake to give in to you about that."

"It would plague Cousin Grace to be everlastingly chaperoning me when I had singing and music elocution lessons, not to mention excursions with a pack of students from Spurbottle for sketching parties and biology and so on. Arabel is arranging all that, and she will go with me, and we shall take picnic lunches on fine days and it will be fun. Cousin Grace hasn't the time."

Nicholas could only agree. His mother was the kindest of women, and she was sincerely fond of Charlotte, but she could not be expected to give up so much time to her.

"Then we can but see how you get along," he said rather vaguely.

It could not be said that he shared Charlotte's alleged intuition, but he was conscious of unease when his mind dwelt on Arabel. An attractive girl, a more than usually interesting girl, but there *was* something faintly disquieting about her. Her eyes were beautiful and unusual, but he had noticed that the pupils were dilated. Her manner sometimes was noticeably dreamy and absent. These might be natural characteristics, though at first when they were talking it had been a palpable effort to her to concentrate on what he was saying. But once having made the effort she was alertly interested.

"I shall get along perfectly," said the confident Charlotte, "for I shall take good care not to antagonize Mrs. Gibson. You do like Arabel, don't you?"

"Very much. It would be impossible not to like her."

"Then don't let Mrs. Gibson stop you being friends with her."

"Why should she want to, you foolish child?"

"I don't know—but promise me. There's the garden party Cosette is giving next month. She has asked us, and I can take a friend, which will be Arabel, of course. She won't be likely to ask Mrs. Gibson or Mr. Herald before she has formally called on them, and I know very well she won't have time before the garden party. Do make a point of seeing as much as you can of Arabel."

"That will be no penance, though I don't fathom your object."

Charlotte for an instant seemed to be out of her depth. "Neither do I—not really. But if she's not well, if there's something wrong with her as Mrs. Gibson hints, mightn't it be a good thing if she talked to you— as a doctor?"

"She has her own family physician, Charlotte."

"Yes—old Galbraith, but he's on the verge of retiring, and from all I've heard, practically in his dotage."

"Scarcely that—before he is sixty." Nicholas laughed tolerantly. "He is not retiring but plans to go to Australia for a while. His married daughter, an only child, lives there, and has pleaded with her parents to pay her an indefinitely long visit. A locum will look after Galbraith's practice while he is away. However, if Arabel wishes to consult me informally, I will give her the best advice I can."

Charlotte said solemnly, "You may laugh, but do you know that makes me feel much better, as though a weight has fallen from my shoulders."


Arabel, meanwhile, had consented to stretch herself out on a sofa in the morning room while her mother sat nearby engaged with the embroidery that was her favorite occupation. Not surprisingly Mrs. Gibson was tired and disinclined for conversation. Arabel glanced through one of the latest novels procured from the nearest circulating library, but it failed to hold her interest, and presently, glancing across at her mother, she saw that her work had fallen to the carpet, and that leaning back in her deep, cushioned chair, she was asleep. This was unusual, for there was scarcely an hour in the day when she was not active.

Arabel had no intention of seeking out Kit when she decided to look for a different book in the library. She had heard him go up the stairs to his study. Ursula did not wake as she left the room, and the library was unoccupied as she had expected. Mrs. Gaskell was a writer of whose work beyond *Cranford* she knew nothing, and there were other books of hers in a uniform edition on one of the top shelves. Standing on the ground, Arabel could not reach this shelf, but there was a short step-ladder, which she mounted. *Cousin Phillis* was a promising title, and she leafed through the book, reading a paragraph here and there with so much absorption that she did not hear the door opening, and she gave a great start when it closed, lurching on the top rung of the steps. Kit, throwing out an arm to catch her, said involuntarily, "That's the second time I've saved you from falling."

"The *second* time!" Arabel echoed, puzzled, and was the more so when his face crimsoned. "What do you mean by the second time?"

"Oh, nothing—it's unimportant." And at this minute the forestalled accident seemed so. What *was* important was the memory of her clinging arms and ardent kiss, and now the pleasurably heady sensation of holding her in a protective embrace against his chest. His senses swam, and nothing had any meaning beyond a rising desire mingled with passion of pity for her. The thought of her had scarcely been absent from his mind since the profoundly disturbing talk with his mother in the early hours of the morning, and thinking of her he had been wretched. He could not doubt the validity of his mother's story. She had not exaggerated her second husband's derangement. The man must have been a madman, dangerous to himself if to nobody else, and there had been his mother before him. With such a history, Arabel's mental stability was bound to be precarious, and what could her future hold for her? How could she be permitted to remain in ignorance, probably to marry and run the risk of bringing children into the world with the same taint? His mother would be forced to tell her the truth. . . . But here Kit's thoughts became blurred, for there was no truth other than that she was in his arms and he loved her.

The admission, instant and undeniable, so shook him that he was speechless, and he gazed into her eyes with a burning question in his. At last he stammered, "Bel . . . you . . . it's the same for you, isn't it?" He saw fear then, a flash that swiftly passed, and simultaneously there was the answer and her lips closer to him and claimed. "Yes," she said.

Neither of them could have told how long that embrace lasted, how long mouth clung to mouth, but it was Arabel who first returned to sanity. She quietly released herself and descended the steps. She sat down on the arm of one of the big, leather-covered chairs and said, "What are we to do about this, Kit?"

"What on earth *can* we do?"

"Only be resolved that it shall never happen again."

"Yes," he agreed.

"To love like this ought to seem wrong, sinful, but it doesn't—only completely natural—and I am not ashamed."

"I should hate you to be ashamed, Bel. It's not your fault or mine."

She said tremulously, "It's as though we have been betrayed, as though the forces of nature that should have made us indifferent to each other, except for an—an unemotional fondness have . . . well, slipped up. There is nothing in our looks to remind us we are brother and sister."

"Half-brother and half-sister," he corrected.

"That does make some difference, of course. I know I strongly resemble my father. . . ."

"No!" he exclaimed.

"But it's true. Ursula has said so more than once. I am not in the least like her. You are, though not in a marked way. If I looked as she looks, or even had the same kind of nature . . . oh, don't you see how automatically safe it would have been for both of us."

He nodded assent. That was the crux of it. The complete lack of similarity; not even a gesture or mannerism common to him or to their mother, whose looks were so essentially English. Arabel's dark, curly hair, unusual green eyes, full dramatic mouth, were oddly non-English, and had her skin been dark she might have looked Spanish or Italian. If she inherited these characteristics from Bernard Gibson, it was little wonder that his father's young widow had been so violently attracted to him and had married him with reckless swiftness knowing nothing of his family's history.

"There's not the slightest sense of kinship," he muttered.

"I suppose that's partly because we've been separated for years, Kit. It would be different if we had been brought up together, shared the same pleasures and troubles. As it is, we are such a surprise to each other."

"The best thing I can do," said Kit, "is to clear out, to go to London earlier than I had planned."

"Is that really essential? It will be a dreadful disappointment to Ursula. I think it would be much more courageous to determine not to be alone together. After all, Charlotte will be here next week. That will make it easier."

"You are more confident of your strength of will than I am of mine. It will be against our inclination to avoid each other."

"Yes, but for years I've been forced to act in a way that's against my inclination."

"Teaching at Seacrest College, do you mean?"

"I detested it there—or I did at first. But I endured and it became tolerable. I learned discipline."

Pity smote Kit, and for the first time he was definitely critical of his mother. She had been wrong to force Arabel into such an imprisoning mould. Of course she had had good reason, but it would have been more natural, more human, had she in her anxiety kept her child with her, watched over her; more especially as that had been Lady Thora's wish.

"What did you mean," asked Arabel suddenly, "when you said you had twice saved me from falling? You meant it, didn't you?"

"Yes . . . I . . . it seemed wiser, or so we thought, not to tell you."

"*We?* And what *is* there to tell me?"

With constraint, since it seemed that sleepwalking might be a symptom of serious mental disorder, Kit told her of the fright she had given him. She listened almost incredulously.

"But how extraordinary. I am convinced I have never done such a thing before. If I had at Seacrest, I should have been seen or heard by somebody."

"My dear, it's quite likely this was an isolated occurrence. Your nerves have been on edge just lately."

"Have they?" Her expression was troubled. "I know Ursula says so, but I wouldn't say I'm a nervy person. It's as though it's physical—something wrong with my health, an organic something, yet Dr. Galbraith says my health is excellent. I do confess though that I've been—well, in quite a state about you—about me; aware that I cared for you—excessively, and not as a sister. I wondered, too, how it was with you."

"Well, now you know." His voice had an edge of roughness.

"It may be wrong, but I do feel a kind of gladness that it happened to us both. If it had been only my madness, I should—I should have hated myself."

Kit sighed, wishing that she had not used the word madness. It had only a slight significance for her. But if she knew . . .

"We must try not to hurt Ursula," said Arabel. "Why should she suffer for our folly? She has had a sad life in many ways, especially in her separation from you. You are far dearer to her than I, which is natural. You are her firstborn, and a son nearly always means more to a woman than a daughter. If you leave sooner than you planned, she will think you are bored, that to be reunited to her is of little consequence to you. As for this sleepwalking, it might be a wise precaution to lock my door each night and to hide the key somewhere. In my sleep I shouldn't be likely to remember where I *had* hidden it."

With the words bravely uttered, the door opened and Ursula came in. Before she could speak, Arabel said,

"No wonder you fell asleep in your chair. Kit has just told me . . . you could have had little rest last night."

"But that was . . . we decided not to . . ." Ursula shot her son a reproachful glance.

"It wasn't intentional," said Kit. "An incautious word on my part. Bel was suspicious, and I had no choice then but to tell her. It *has* rather scared her, though."

"*Has* it, Arabel? But I am sure you have no cause for alarm. Neither you nor I are accustomed to such a heavy, elaborate dinner as we were given last evening. It must have upset your digestion, and then the heat as well . . . We need a thunderstorm to clear the air."

"If we get one," said Arabel, "I must take care not to be caught outdoors; that drenching I had seems to have started all the trouble, for I've not been really well since."

"You need a tonic, dear. To tell the truth I haven't much faith in Dr. Galbraith's mixtures. I shall study my herbal book and blend something for you. Nature's cures are better than these modern drugs. Mrs. Digby agrees with me. We had quite an interesting conversation last evening. She has a recipe for a spring medicine which purifies the blood. It has been handed down in her family for generations. I must coax her to tell me the ingredients."

"I'd rather stop taking all medicines, even herbal ones," Arabel replied, and then glancing at the clock, she said, "Nicholas and Charlotte should soon be back from their drive, and then we can have tea."

"I didn't want you to sleep in a different wing. You would have been so far away from the rest of us at night, so I hope you will be comfortable here in Lady Thora's suite. All the guest rooms are rather small, unsuitable for a long stay. These rooms have just been redecorated, and it's an advantage to have your own bathroom and little sitting room."

Arabel, as she went from room to room with Charlotte at her heels, refrained from mentioning that Lady Thora had died here, and although Charlotte knew that it must have been so, it was not a fact that troubled her. She would have said reasonably that old people, many people, had died as well as lived in all old houses. She stood in the center of the bedroom and looked around her with delight, admiring the cream and pink decor that Arabel thought insipid.

"It's lovely," Charlotte said, "and I shall feel very grand having a sitting room of my own."

"I shall expect you to study in it," Arabel said, reverting momentarily to the embryo schoolmistress of Seacrest College.

"I promise you I will. I'd hate to be unappreciative of all you have planned for me."

In the small sitting room there was a glass-fronted bookcase waiting for Charlotte's books to fill it, chairs covered with gay chintz, an escritoire of eighteenth-century design, painted with garlands of roses, and on the mantelpiece a procession of china animals, all in pairs as though lined up to enter an invisible ark.

"These must have been hers," Charlotte said, lightly touching a lamb's china crinkled fleece.

"Yes. Lady Thora was very fond of them, I remember. She had, perhaps, a rather childish taste."

"But according to Cosette Wentworth, who knew her quite well, she was a rather childish person—childish but sweet. Cosette said she gave the impression of having no will of her own."

"She may have been deceptive in that way." Involuntarily Arabel thought of the secret visit to the solicitor in London. Lady Thora had then certainly carried out her own wishes.

Charlotte wondered. Cosette had said that in her opinion Ursula had overruled her employer and that the constant visits abroad were undertaken more because the housekeeper enjoyed foreign travel than for any hope that Lady Thora's health would benefit by them. Cosette, after all, might be prejudiced, for she was one of the few people who did not like Mrs. Gibson—Charlotte being another.

"Was this her desk?" Charlotte asked.

"Yes. She wrote her letters at it, and Ursula says it was so crammed with an accumulation of papers that it would hardly close." Briefly Arabel described how by chance Lady Thora's second will, leaving everything to her, had been found.

Charlotte unlocked the front of the little desk and examined it with pleasure. It had, she thought, everything to make it perfect: small drawers with minute, mother-of-pearl handles, slender pigeonholes containing writing paper and envelopes, a mother-of-pearl inkwell, pens and pencils, a blotter framed in pale leather, and even a supply of stamps in a box painted with roses to match the desk. Charlotte sat down at it.

"I shall love writing here, working here," she said. "My mother insists that I must continue with my German and French and Italian lessons, and Cousin Grace has made inquiries and has been told of a local tutor who takes a few advanced pupils for classes at his home. I only hope I'm sufficiently advanced, for his other pupils are older than I. It would be mortifying if he refused to accept me."

"Oh, I'm sure he won't. At Seacrest, languages and history were your special subjects. I am glad you are keen to work, for you mustn't waste this year. Next year you will be coming out, won't you?"

"I suppose so, unofficially, anyway, and presented the following spring. It all seems rather pointless. Languages may be useful, but nobody will think history important, though it means such a lot to me . . . the magic of it . . . the sense of the past . . . kinship with a multitude of people known to me, though I am not known to them. I wish I could go to Girton to try for a history degree, but neither Father nor Mother will hear of it. They detest bluestockings and just want me to have nice manners, good looks, accomplishments, and of course charm, though I doubt if one can acquire charm. You either have it or you don't have it."

"No need to despair." Standing by the desk, which, so delicately painted, so perfect in every minute detail, typified the France of an earlier day, which had ended in the bloody welter of the Revolution, Arabel reflected how little charm and highbred delicacy had served too many lovely women. This pretty toy might have belonged to one who had met a violent death. She lightly touched Charlotte's fair, bent head, and the girl raised it to smile up at her. "You won't have to work to acquire grace and pretty manners," Arabel said, and she might have added—as I did.

Although the past was already dreamlike, she would never forget it. All that artificial deference to a convention-bound headmistress, all the willingness to step into the breach when senior mistresses were sick or demanded unscheduled leave of absence, how she had secretly revolted, yet had been determined to advance herself. Even her friendship with Charlotte, the carefully orthodox friendship of the youngest member of the staff with a socially important pupil, had perhaps in the beginning had its roots in self-aggrandizement, though finally she had become very fond of Charlotte. If it was ironical to realize that she need not have exerted herself to win favor, since Lady Thora's whim had made advancement in the scholastic world completely unimportant, it was even more ironical to reflect that this enormous change in her life had already brought her near to disaster. Had she stayed on at Seacrest College, she and Kit might not have met again for years—if ever.

Although she had spoken with such resolution of discipline and self-control, she knew how difficult this would be. Both Kit and she ought to find other interests, she thought desperately, and hardly heard what Charlotte was saying.

"Your brother writes historical novels, doesn't he? But his first book isn't yet published, he told me. Do you think I might dare to ask him if I could read the manuscript? Would he be angry?"

"Of course not." Arabel vaguely gathered the drift of this.

"He must have a rough copy, mustn't he?"

"Why yes, I suppose so."

Arabel, now attentive, looked down into the flushed, upturned face. A pretty face that had changed even in the last few weeks, losing something of its schoolgirl chubbiness that the Seacrest diet of suet puddings, thick slabs of bread and butter, and mounds of potatoes had encouraged.

Charlotte, Arabel realized, was impressionable, and men balked of love were prone to seek consolation. A genuine love of the same subject might draw Kit toward this engaging child, who was too young to come to any permanent harm through a first, innocent fancy for a clever and attractive young man. If she, Arabel, had any sense, she would welcome this possibility.

Fighting down pain and desolation, she said, "I am sure if there is such a copy, Kit will lend it to you. Ask him, of course, Charlotte. He is a very kind person, and in any case why *should* he be angry? It's much more likely that he will be flattered."

"Do you really think so? Then I will." The color deepened in Charlotte's cheeks, and her eyes were dreamy.

# CHAPTER 8

Charlotte, easily pleased, and very happy to be with Arabel, speedily settled down at Troy Court. Having made her faltering request to Kit, she was overjoyed when he said readily that certainly since she was so interested she could read the rough copy of his soon-to-be-published book. On second thoughts it occurred to him that he could do even better than that for her. His publisher had sent him a spare set of galley proofs, which would be far easier to read than his handwriting.

Charlotte gazed with wonder at the long slips Kit had clipped together which, when she started to read, soon uncoiled and tended to wrap themselves around her.

The days for Charlotte were full of occupations and diversions. Arabel had already arranged for her to attend private classes for languages three times a week; masters of music, singing, drawing, and painting would call at Troy Court. Mrs. Gibson set her lips disapprovingly, but said nothing when she discovered that music lessons would be given in the large drawing room where there was a grand piano. Arabel could not see that this would inconvenience anyone. The room was so vast that it was scarcely ever used except for formal entertainment. It would be good for the piano to be used regularly, and in the autumn and winter fires had to be lighted as in most of the other rooms; therefore it would give nobody any extra work because Charlotte needed a warm room in which to practice.

Neither Mrs. Gibson nor Charlotte expressed an open dislike for each other, and they behaved with impeccable correctness, but Charlotte's opinion was unaltered, and Mrs. Gibson remarked to Kit that the girl had been so spoiled that she took everything for granted and behaved as though Troy Court were her home.

"But surely that's how you would want her to behave since she is to stay here for months," Kit said, slightly amused but not surprised, for it was his belief that older women rarely liked young ones.

"If it had come about gradually, yes; but Charlotte has been here less than a week, and as a matter of course she is making excessive demands on Arabel's time."

"Bel doesn't seem to mind, does she?"

"No, but she isn't really up to being dragged hither and thither at that spoiled child's whims. I've encouraged Arabel to keep early hours, which I am sure are essential to her health, but Charlotte says she had enough of that at Seacrest, and although she says goodnight when I suggest it is time we all retired, she does no more than get into her dressing gown and then settles herself in the Chinese room to chatter to Arabel for hours. It's sometimes nearly midnight before she leaves her. However, I have made Arabel promise to take her tisane immediately after she has had her bath; this always makes her sleepy, and it's to be hoped when Charlotte sees it is only with an effort that she keeps her eyes open, she will have sufficient consideration to leave her."

Kit privately thought that his mother was being needlessly fussy, though it was natural enough as she was in a state of perpetual anxiety about Arabel. But Charlotte's young and lighthearted companionship was probably good for her and diverted her thoughts. His poor girl, he thought compassionately—they could not be particularly happy thoughts; and no more were his. It was fiendish ill-fortune that this irresistible attraction had sprung up between them, for there was no way out for either of them. He, thwarted though he was, suffered less than Arabel, who had never before been in love and under these circumstances found it terrifying. Kit, who, though sincere, had a certain cynical wisdom, knew that with the passing of time such intense emotion, such strong desire being starved, was bound to wane, though a scar would be left on his consciousness and hers. The chief trouble was that at the moment he rebelled against the imposed self-denial. Arabel avoided him as much as she could, and she and Charlotte were rarely apart, but nonetheless she was a maddening temptation to him, and in weaker moments it seemed unnecessary to deny himself. To a limited extent at least they could make each other happy, and who would suffer for it? Nobody would even suspect it. When Kit thought of Arabel's future he was wretched for her. She had money and a beautiful home, but she was doomed to lifelong loneliness, for how could his mother allow her to marry in ignorance of her heritage? Kit, who had the gift of living in the present, would, had Arabel been weakly compliant, have taken what happiness he could from the immediate hour, but she was bent on protecting them both from what to her should seem wicked and unnatural and was the more bewildering because it didn't.

Sometimes Kit would have given much to leave Troy Court, though it was an ideal place in which to work, but the rooms in London were not yet vacant, and it was true, as Arabel said, that if he departed before they were ready, his mother would be bitterly disappointed, and it would be very difficult to provide a plausible reason for it. The chief solace from his point of view was that he was able, for long hours at a time, to lose himself in his work. Once swept back in time to the reign of Queen Anne, and steeped in the complexities that had tormented her, he could forget his own.

Charlotte was in little doubt that Arabel's mother disapproved of her, but this only amused her. Padding down the long passage, clad in a dressing gown and with her feet in soft-soled slippers, she collided with Mrs. Gibson, who was emerging from the Chinese room. Charlotte dropped a sheaf of the book proofs that dangled in streamers over her arm, and as she stooped to gather them up, Mrs. Gibson said, "I have just put Arabel's tisane, her nightcap as we call it, on the table beside her bed. She is still in the bath, but when she comes out, please ask her to take the tisane while it is hot. It's beneficial for the nerves and induces sleep."

"I'll tell her," Charlotte promised, moving toward the door of the Chinese room. "Good-night, Mrs. Gibson."

"Good-night, my dear." The older woman's pride would not permit her to appeal to Charlotte to stay only a brief while in Arabel's room. She had already expressed her views about the undesirability of late hours.

Charlotte was stretched comfortably on the chaise lounge when Arabel came out of the bathroom. "This book of Kit's is wonderful," she said. "Aren't you curious to read it?"

"Very, but it will be published in a few weeks, and I shall get a much better impression of it than trying to concentrate on those endless streamers, which must be most confusing."

"Not really, not when you get used to them. It's a most exciting, colorful story."

"That's what is expected of historical romance."

"You do take it calmly, Arabel. Aren't you terribly proud to have such a gifted brother?"

"I am indeed." How easy it was to speak lightly, and to show no more than a casual, easy affection. Everyone could act when they had to, Arabel supposed bitterly, yet if she and Kit were alone together for no more than five minutes, their hands clung, and there would be the swift, ardent caress for which both were burningly eager. There were times when a vast weariness swept over Arabel, and she felt years older than nineteen. Too much had happened in too short a time. She did not believe that she was physically ill as her mother hinted, but emotionally it was as though she was being torn asunder.

Charlotte indicated the glass on the bedside table that Mrs. Gibson had covered with a saucer. "Your mother told me to remind you to drink it while it was hot."

"It's generally too hot when Ursula brings it and I have to let it cool; she has the most fantastic faith in these herbal remedies for minor aches and ills and is extremely mysterious about them; nobody must know what they contain. This nightly tisane has tasted rather different just lately; it's probably stronger."

Arabel sipped the drink, and glancing at her, Charlotte was aware of a wanness in the vivid face she so much admired. The high cheekbones were slightly more prominent, and the tip-tilted green eyes looked very large. Something *was* wrong with Arabel, concluded Charlotte, but she had no idea what it could be.

"Do you mind if I stay for a little while?" she asked. "It's lovely to be with you, with nobody to intrude on us."

"Of course I don't mind. We can both read. I am still only halfway through Mrs. Gaskell's *Cousin Phillis.*"

Arabel, having swallowed the content of the glass, got into bed, moved the candle so that the light fell upon the page of her book, and there was contented silence. But within a very short time her book fell to the floor, and by her heavy breathing Charlotte realized she was already asleep. If this was due to Mrs. Gibson's tisane it had had a swift effect. Charlotte continued to read, and was soon so engrossed that for a while she forgot everything else. An hour or more sped by unnoticed. Then she was disturbed by Arabel's murmuring voice, and setting aside the proofs, she glanced toward the bed. Arabel was sitting up, and although her murmuring voice was agitated, it was impossible to distinguish what she said. The candle was too near the bed thought Charlotte. It really wasn't safe if one fell suddenly asleep without snuffing it, especially if Arabel was often as restless as this.

She was about to make some attempt to soothe her friend, to coax her to lie down again and put out the candle, when Arabel astonished her by casting off the blankets with an impatient, impetuous movement, and then rose from the bed. The startled Charlotte watched her in silence. Arabel stood for a few moments beside the bed, looking down at it with an expression so strangely mournful that Charlotte was spellbound and felt unable to move. Then with a deep sigh Arabel turned away toward the window, and looking ghostlike and unreal in her trailing nightgown, she walked unsteadily across the room and without hesitation opened the window. It was a chilly night and rain was falling, a strong wind blew the silk curtains aside, candle flames leaped upward. Not before this had Charlotte consciously noticed that the windows were so long and so low that they were almost even with the floor. Arabel raised one foot and it rested on the edge of the window frame; she swayed forward and the wind caught her hair and swirled it around her face.

For Charlotte, the spell that had bound her broke and, as she afterward reflected, not a moment too soon. In a rush she was across the room and her arms were flung about Arabel's waist. She was by far the stronger, by far the most robust, which was as well, since the still unconscious Arabel fought her convulsively; but then, suddenly, she sagged in Charlotte's arms, and the girl half-dragged, half-led her away from the window. At the same instant, normal life and intelligence dawned in Arabel's eyes. She gazed, first into Charlotte's face and then around the room in complete bewilderment. "What in the world . . . ? What has happened?" she demanded.

"I don't exactly know." Charlotte spoke shakily. "I think you must have been sleepwalking."

As though sleep had not touched her for hours and was far from her now, Arabel observed the glittering candles, the wide-open window and Charlotte's pale, scared face.

"Did I open that?" she asked, indicating the window.

"Yes, just now."

"It must have been a hard job. I bolted it earlier, top and bottom, and the bolts were very stiff."

"It wasn't bolted, Arabel, of that I am quite certain. I watched you—you only lifted the latch."

"But I could swear . . . Charlotte, I couldn't have been mistaken. Ever since I was told I walked in my sleep, I've been frightened of that window, and I've bolted it. One could so easily walk out of it into noth-ingness . . . as she did."

"As she . . . you mean the Chinese bride of years and years ago?"

"She would have died, really died, if she had lived out her natural span, but as it is, I sometimes think she is still very much alive, and that she influences me."

"Oh, Arabel, no!"

"Not consciously, not maliciously, poor little thing, but her unhappiness still lingers here. Oh, it may be all fancy." In a matter-of-fact way, Arabel crossed the room and snuffed out the candle on the bedside table. "An oil lamp would really be safer," she remarked.

"Nothing is safe if you . . . you said you walked in your sleep before."

"Only once, so far as I know, and I remember noth-ing about it. That time it seems I walked down the stairs and should have fallen down then if Kit had not caught me. Oh, Charlotte, I'm sorry about this. It must have frightened you."

"Well, it did, of course, but how could you help it?

I'm thankful I was here. That window . . . ," and Charlotte repressed a sob.

"I really did bolt it," Arabel insisted. "I've been nervous myself, ever since I was told about the sleep-walking."

"But you never did anything of the kind at Seacrest. There were night cleaners . . . they would have seen you if you had. As for the window, perhaps somebody opened it after you bolted it."

"That must have been it, though it was a foolish thing for a maid to do with the rain lashing in. I suppose the girl realized as much and closed it again, not thinking to shoot the bolts."

But it needn't have been a maid; thought Charlotte, terrified of a flashing suspicion but unable to dismiss it. Mrs. Gibson had been in the room while Arabel was taking her bath, and if she, Charlotte, had not been there, a fatal accident would almost certainly have occurred. She shuddered and clung to her friend. "You must have bars put across," she said urgently.

"That would take a little time, but I can tell one of the gardeners to fix a wire netting outside. It could be done tomorrow. I shall say that I need the air, but that the window when open is too low for safety. It will sound quite natural, don't you think?"

"Yes. Do you want me to keep quiet about this?"

"Oh, Charlotte, please. Ursula and Kit both worry . . . Ursula especially, and she watches me, guards me . . . of course with the best intentions, but it irks me."

"I won't say a word," Charlotte promised. "I do understand; it must be horrible to feel that someone's eyes are always on you."

"It is, and yet . . . poor Ursula . . . it's perfectly natural . . ."

There was a brief silence before Charlotte nerved herself to say, "Those herbal drinks . . . isn't it possible they don't agree with you? They may have a soothing effect upon most people, but you could be the exception. Need you take them, Arabel?"

"My mother would be so hurt and vexed if I refused, and besides . . . she'd think of something else for me to take."

"Then don't tell her. That would be the easiest way. Throw the stuff away, and just for a few nights at least, see how you sleep without anything to help you. Herbal or not, those tisanes must be a kind of drug. How do you feel now? I read or heard it was dangerous to wake anyone walking in their sleep, but what else could I do?"

"Nothing of course, and it has done me no harm. If you hadn't been here . . . oh Charlotte!"

"I know. What a mercy I ignored your mother's wishes about not staying long in your room at nights. In the ordinary way I should have left for my own, but I became absorbed in Kit's book and forgot the time passing."

"You must go now, though," said Arabel, "or you will get no sleep at all. You needn't worry about me. Look, if you're nervous, we can, between us, pull that bureau over and put it before the window. It'll be quite safe, for I could never move it away on my own. I shall have to wake you early to help me put it back in its place."

"Let me sleep on this chaise longue, or even turn in with you," Charlotte pleaded. "It won't matter if Bessie finds me here when she brings the early tea. I can say I was lonely or had a bad dream."

To this Arabel agreed and with secret relief. The four-poster easily accommodated them both, and Arabel soon fell asleep again. Charlotte stayed awake for considerably longer, tormented by her troubled thoughts. Was she wicked to have such terrible suspicions? She had distrusted Ursula Gibson from the first, though there was nothing but an irrational, intuitive dislike to support such distrust; that, and the vague perplexity because nothing in Mrs. Gibson's attitude tallied with her near neglect while Arabel was at Seacrest. Charlotte could not now remember who had said in her hearing that if Arabel died before she was twenty-one Mrs. Gibson inherited Troy Court and all that Lady Thora had left to Arabel, but it seemed to be generally known. Would Mrs. Gibson be glad if Arabel died? No doubt a scheming and heartless person would. Mrs. Gibson seemed to be neither, but people could pretend, could disguise their characters. Who could tell what those alleged soothing herbal drinks contained? Some drug, perhaps, that, far from soothing, excited and distressed and caused delirious dreams.

Charlotte fully believed that Arabel had, as she declared, bolted the window, and while she was in her bath Mrs. Gibson, who had brought the tisane to her room, had had the opportunity to unbolt it. Could she possibly have hoped that if she walked in her sleep again, her fate might be a repetition of the Chinese bride of generations ago?

Well, at least so far as the window was concerned, precautions could be taken. It was on this relieved thought that Charlotte finally fell asleep.


Meeting Mrs. Gibson the next day, closely, silently observing her, Charlotte was obliged to admit that her nebulous suspicions were fantastic, for her warm benevolence was unforced, and when Arabel blandly assured her that she had slept well, she appeared to be delighted. She had put a little extra something into last night's tisane, Mrs. Gibson confessed, the "little something" being of course completely harmless.

That afternoon, rather to Charlotte's surprise, Cosette Wentworth called on Mrs. Gibson and Arabel. She apologized sweetly for the delay in so doing, but put this down to having had a multitude of social engagements since returning from the Continent. Now she hoped that both Mrs. Gibson and her daughter would be among the guests at the garden party she was giving the following week. If this did not allow Mrs. Gibson time to return her call, could they not agree to forego ceremony? Cosette's manner was very winning, and although Charlotte knew that she was not one of Mrs. Gibson's admirers, but considered her a domineering upstart, it was impossible to detect this; nor did she betray relief, but only polite regret, when Ursula said that on the day of the garden party she and Kit would be in London. Kit had arranged to see his publisher on that day, and she had one or two appointments in London to which she must attend. She disliked traveling alone and would be glad of her son's company, said Ursula.

Cosette said then that she hoped Arabel would accompany Charlotte, whereupon Charlotte accepted the invitation for both of them, giving Mrs. Gibson no time to raise an objection if such was in her mind.

"Cousin Grace will chaperon us both," she said. "It will be lovely. I adore a garden party, partly I suppose because one is in terror in case it rains and is so buoyed up if it doesn't."

"If it rains there will be an inside party," Cosette said. "It's rather late in the year for an outside one and slightly disappointing without the traditional strawberries and cream, but I've thought of one or two sideshows to liven things up—a really famous fortune-teller, for one thing. She was pointed out to us at Epsom on Derby day, and she read my hand and was so amazingly good that I engaged her then and there for my September garden party. And in fact she gave me the date for it, vowing that it would be warm and sunny."

"My dear Mrs. Wentworth, do you really believe in such absurdity as fortune-telling?" Ursula inquired.

Cosette wrinkled her pert and pretty nose as though in thought. "I'm not sure—I have an open mind. This woman—she calls herself Zillah—is impressive, and she told me a few surprising things—how many children I had, and how Nancy nearly died of croup, and she described my wedding dress as unusual and not pure white, which was true, for I look ghastly in white and chose a deep cream satin. I was, of course, a complete stranger to her, so how could she have known such things?"

Mrs. Gibson looked mildly skeptical. "I suspect these clever frauds take trouble to identify those who consult them, and probably know by sight most people who are of any account. You, Mrs. Wentworth, are a well-known figure in society, and items of news appear in the current journals. I have no doubt your wedding dress has been described more than once."

"That seems rather farfetched," Cosette commented. "Zillah could not have had the slightest idea I intended to patronize her, for it was only on impulse that I did, and when one considers the hundreds of people at the Derby, she couldn't possibly know all their histories."

"I dare say she makes a good many blunders in the case of obscure people." And then Ursula smiled kindly and said, "But it is unkind to try to spoil the amusement the woman must have given you, though if it does rain on the day of the garden party it will make her look very foolish."

Cosette agreed that it would, but her faith in the Derby seeress was evidently firm, and when the visitor had left, Ursula commented disparagingly on this. It was extraordinary to find anyone of education so gullible. But Mrs. Gibson, reflected Charlotte with satisfaction, could herself be gullible, for it obviously did not occur to her that Arabel could deceive her and only pretend to take the herbal draught that was left by her bedside each night; nor did she suspect that Charlotte forced herself to stay awake and then when she judged it safe, slipped noiselessly into Arabel's room and slept in the big four-poster.

Arabel gave her own instructions to a gardener about the wire netting, and this, to Charlotte's surprise, was not detected. The wire had a fine mesh, and Arabel said nothing about it. As she told Charlotte, she was not clever at subterfuge, and although she would, if questioned, give the explanation they had decided upon, she preferred not to refer to it of her own accord. Her mother rarely entered her room during the daytime, and the curtains were drawn when she paid her customary visit last thing at night.

"After all, she mightn't believe me," Arabel explained. "And if she suspected I had walked in my sleep again, it would worry her." She felt guilty over the trifling conspiracy, harmless though it was; but there was now no necessity to bolt the window, and as she invariably locked her door at night. Charlotte's presence in her room was not suspected. "Though it isn't good for you to make yourself stay awake in order to be with me," she said, "and I truly don't think it's necessary. I feel quite confident in my own mind that I shall not repeat that dramatic, somnambulist act, for I believe you were right as to the cause of it. Poor Ursula's famous herbal remedies don't agree with me, however beneficial they may be generally. The last few nights have been wonderful. No tisane, but hours and hours of dreamless sleep."

"You look much better," Charlotte said with satisfaction, and it was true that Arabel's eyes were no longer shadowed.

"I feel tremendously better. For weeks now I've been dreamy and lethargic in the daytime, which was very unusual. I was brisk enough when I was at Seacrest. I should soon have been lectured if I had been otherwise."

Charlotte said hesitantly, "I do wish you would talk to Nicholas about the sleepwalking. He wouldn't fuss you, I'm sure, and he might be able to give you some explanations."

"But why should I worry him since I'm convinced it is all over?"

"It wouldn't worry him in the way of being bored. He—well, he likes you very much and is interested in all that concerns you. You're not blind, Arabel, you must see it for yourself."

"Must I?" Arabel laughed, though with a shade of unease. "You, perhaps, see too much for your age, Charlotte, or rather imagine too much."

In some ways, thought Charlotte, it would be a relief to be sure that she *was* wildly imaginative, for there were times when she felt herself to be positively wicked. How *could* she have such really horrible suspicions about one so seemingly kind and considerate as Mrs. Gibson? Could these have simply grown upon her because she knew that Arabel's mother did not really approve of her as a permanent visitor at Troy Court? Charlotte was convinced that the antagonism was mutual, but the appearance of liking and cordiality between them was well maintained, and neither Kit nor Arabel suspected that it was anything but sincere.

Charlotte had now read the proofs of Kit's first book, and she returned them with comments that were so intelligent and thoughtful that he was surprised and impressed. Although he had been half in earnest when he said that men were not drawn to clever women, he was not averse to Charlotte's type of cleverness, which only made her interest in his work the more agreeable.

"She's an unusual girl," he told Arabel, "and has a real feeling for history; the people of those days live for her still. Her conclusions are sound too, though we're not always in agreement. For instance, I see Catherine of Braganza as a most unhappy woman, but Charlotte takes the opposite viewpoint. She thinks that as Catherine loved Charles with single-minded intensity, she was, finally, content with the little he gave her, though she denies that it *was* little. He was consistently unfaithful to her, but she was his wife, and although she was childless and he badly wanted a son born in wedlock, he would not take any steps to rid himself of her. He was kind to her; he protected her and vindicated her when that scoundrel Oates did his utmost to ruin her. . . ."

"I suppose it did add up to a good deal," Arabel said, "and he probably loved her in his way."

"A poor way, when one considers the fever and the torment and the glory that love can be."

"If Catherine of Braganza outstripped the torment and the fever of it she was fortunate," Arabel said, looking down upon his hand, which was folded over hers.

They were alone, as seldom happened, lingering over a late breakfast. Both had slept beyond the accustomed hour—Kit, because he had been working until between two and three o'clock, Arabel, because eight or nine hour's sleep were none too many for her—she was catching up on all she had missed for months. Now Mrs. Gibson was having her morning consultation with the housekeeper, waging the usual veiled, polite battle with a successor who was as resolved as was Ursula to conduct the household management in her own way. From the drawing room there came the sound of scales and arpeggios as Charlotte put in an hour's pianoforte practice.

"From the look of you," said Kit, "our impossible situation doesn't weigh heavily upon you. During the last few days you have thrown off that air of fragile delicacy that worried me as much as it worried our mamma."

"You don't seem altogether pleased by the improvement. You've been glooming all through breakfast, though if I expected signs of distress due to my disturbing effect on you, I might well be peevish over your excellent appetite. Porridge, a kipper, three rashers of bacon, two eggs, toast, marmalade, and three cups of coffee. It doesn't suggest a hopeless and forbidden passion."

"How *can* you treat it as a joke?" he asked reproachfully.

"Because if I didn't—if I didn't, Kit, I should be in despair."

"Darling Bel!"

"What can we do but try to treat it lightly? Otherwise what we feel for each other could drag us down into a labyrinth of evil," she said unhappily.

"I don't agree. Where's the harm in taking what pleasure and happiness is possible? Sometimes I feel that if I could have one whole day alone with you, I could live on the memory of it for a year. If only you could come to London with me tomorrow, and we could persuade Mother to show up at Cosette's party in your stead."

"Nothing would persuade her to alter her plans. Surely you know she would far, far rather be with you than at any party. Besides, even if she and I did change places, it would be dangerous . . . and to me frightening."

"Because you don't trust yourself?"

"I trust neither of us."

"But Bel, I assure you."

She shook her head and strove to withdraw her hand from his. "Oh Kit, why will you persist in deceiving yourself? You won't call—this—by its right name—an incestuous love. You prefer to think of it as romantic and harmless, denying that it could destroy us. I know enough, I've read enough, to realize how easy it would be to slip into a secret intrigue, and a few hours alone together, secure from intrusion, might see the beginning of it."

"You misjudge me, darling. I can be strong for both of us, and I would never allow . . . well, allow anything to occur that you would afterward regret. But I have a great longing to know you better, which is impossible when I rarely have you to myself for half an hour. Why shouldn't I take you up to London some day soon— openly, saying that I plan to show you over the chambers I shall be occupying next month? Wouldn't it be natural for you to help choose materials for fresh curtains and cushions?"

"Perfectly natural, but Ursula would consider she was the right person to look after you in that way, and she would be extremely upset if you asked me instead of her."

Kit sighed. "Fond though I am of her, I'm bound to say she's a possessive woman."

"Most mothers are, I expect, where sons are concerned. Daughters seem to be different. It's callous the way in which many of them are married off to the first eligible man who offers for them. At least I don't have to fear that. I shall be my own mistress, free to marry or not, as I choose."

"You are not free, nor am I, since we are . . . like this."

He rose impetuously and drew her to her feet. They kissed lingeringly, once, and then Arabel drew away. On previous occasions there had, she realized, been more emotion, and more reluctance on her part to withdraw from an embrace, and the sense of guilt had been only because she forced herself to remember their near relationship. In the ordinary way it would not be particularly shameful to enjoy an emotional love affair that did not necessarily culminate in marriage. From all she had heard, many girls enjoyed what they described as "flutters." This was her first experience of lovemaking, a delayed experience since she was nearly twenty years of age, but in spite of the cloistered life at Seacrest, she was endowed with a certain intuitive wisdom.

Perhaps such first love, even when there were no barriers, was rarely lasting. It was too abrupt, too dazzling, too experimental. She was attracted to Kit, she found it impossible to think of him as a brother, but wasn't the danger of their association, the ever-present knowledge that it was forbidden fruit, a spice that enhanced it? Wasn't this part of its fascination?

Such self-questioning was not without humiliation, for only a week or so ago, she had been persuaded that unnatural though it might be, Kit was the love of her life. But she had been incapable then of rational judgment. Insomnia, the horrible sleepwalking, had demoralized her; she had been constantly dazed and feverish and restlessly weary.

When Kit spoke of the torment and the glory of love, he spoke like a poet, or at all events as a writer might be expected to speak. She, Arabel supposed, was more mundane. A fever was a fever, and it should be starved if one intended to recover from it. She knew now that she did so intend.

She gazed at Kit, already almost her lost love, with a sad regret that he naturally failed to understand. It would have shocked him that a girl of less than twenty years old could be so cynically wise. Cynicism was for men, not for women, to whom love was the most overwhelming experience in life. He agreed with the poet whose views regarding the respective involvement of the sexes had recently been set to music: "It's half the world to me, dear, and all the world to you."

Poor darling, he thought, for whom love in its entirety was out of the question. She was doomed and as yet had no suspicion of it, and his love, which would chivalrously content itself with harmless caresses, was the only type of love in which she would ever dare to indulge. Finally she was bound to discover the truth about herself, and she would realize that she could never give herself in love or marriage to any man. Then, handicapped, leashed by the taint in her blood, how grateful she would be for him, who would always be in the background of her life, understanding and consoling. Even when he married, and he supposed he would marry in years to come, this would not alter the romantic, tender "might have been" that neither of them would ever wish to forget.

# CHAPTER 9

On the day of the garden party at Tower House it was so hot and so sunny that it could have been midsummer. Zillah, the seeress, must be feeling smugly pleased with herself, Kit remarked, as he and his mother drove off to the station to catch the train to Waterloo.

"I wonder if there *is* anything in precognition," said Charlotte. "I mean, I wonder if it's possible."

"I shouldn't think so as regards the English weather," Arabel replied. "That prognostication could have been only a gamble, though not so risky as some, for September is often a much better month than July and August. The times I've been sorry for people on August bank holiday, determined to have a day at the sea at any cost, and generally facing leaden skies and heavy showers, if nothing worse."

With Ursula away, both girls felt a luxurious sense of relaxed leisure. They could do exactly as they liked for the entire morning, have luncheon alone together, and then spend at least an hour preparing for the party before Mrs. Digby and Nicholas called to take them to Tower House. For this occasion, Arabel was discarding deep mourning and was wearing a new and becoming gown of silver-gray taffeta shot with lilac. Most of Lady Thora's jewels had been bequeathed to her, but they were lodged in the bank and would not be handed over to her until her twenty-first birthday. Fortunately she was content with the silver filigree necklace and brooch and bracelet, which were the only elegant trinkets she possessed. Nothing could look prettier with her new gown and the picture hat of gray chiffon with its drooping brim. Charlotte's dress was of pale silk muslin with a tiny pillbox hat composed of rose petals. The two girls ran in and out of each other's rooms, put finishing touches to their toilets, laughed and chattered, both wondering why there should be this sense of restrictions removed, for Mrs. Gibson never interfered with their pleasures or plans. But she was everlastingly "hovering," thought Charlotte, and one could be aware of disapproval even if it was not uttered.

When Mrs. Digby and Nicholas arrived from Green Lawns, both Arabel and Charlotte were duly admired, and they set off gaily in the Digbys' landau, which was large enough comfortably to accommodate three crinolines. Nicholas was touched and amused by Arabel's ill-concealed excitement, as she remarked that she had never before been a guest at a big party of any kind, unless one put school prizegiving parties into this category. Today she seemed even younger than Charlotte, to whom such diversions were not unknown.

"Though I expect this party will be quite special," Charlotte said. "Cosette is imaginative and inventive and spares no pains."

"No money either," Mrs. Digby supplemented, her thoughts dwelling somewhat wistfully on Cosette's prodigality. The Digbys were comfortably off, but this seemed almost poverty compared with the half-million reputed to have been settled on Cosette at the time of her marriage.

Tower House was an immense, not particularly beautiful structure, but the grounds were exquisite and had been designed by a world-famous landscape gardener; the fact that they were supremely artificial only added to the novelty of miniature dells and flower-gammed hillocks, twisting avenues, and rock gardens and a delightful bird sanctuary. There was a lake upon which brightly colored pleasure boats floated; summer houses and secluded nooks were provided with rustic seats; a little stream flowed over stones so white that they looked as though they had been scrubbed, and it was spanned by an ornamental bridge. As well, there were tennis courts, croquet lawns, and yew hedges forming a maze. An enormous marquee had been set up and each guest was presented with a printed program, setting forth the various entertainments and competitions. A band was playing, flags were flying. Arabel was entranced. It occurred to her that Cosette must certainly have believed implicitly in the gypsy's promise that the day would be ideally summerlike, for how could all these temporary structures have been dismantled at short notice, and indoor amusement provided instead?

It came about quite naturally that she and Nicholas spent most of the afternoon together. Mrs. Digby and Charlotte were already friendly with several of the guests and were soon sauntering around with them, and although Charlotte would have included Arabel, it was easy for Nicholas to detach her. They explored the grounds together, rowed out on the lake to the minute island in the center of it, though this afforded no landing, being merely a large clump of flowering shrubs, stepped gingerly within the yew maze, and with difficulty found their way out again. In these activities they were joined by several others, most of whom only knew Arabel by name and repute and now subjected her to discreetly curious inspection. But she was hardened to this. She and her mother had been called upon by one or two families who did not wish to offend the Digbys, who were evidently so friendly with them, but it would be a long time before they were generally accepted.

The fortune-teller's tent had been set up in a conspicuous position, and, one by one, guests of both sexes half-ashamedly stole in to consult her. Nicholas had no curiosity and certainly no belief in the seeress, and said that if he had, it would be a reason for avoiding her, as he could imagine nothing more disconcerting than to be given a glimpse into the future. But Arabel, who was intrigued, was determined to hear anything the seeress could tell her. Nicholas waited for her, as she lifted the flap of the tent and entered.

She had formed no clear idea of what she might expect to see. The interior of the tent was dim, and, dazzled by the brilliant sunshine without, she could at first see nothing distinctly; when she did, she was astonished by the simplicity of the furniture. There was no gaudy semi-Oriental exuberance, only a deal kitchen table and two wooden chairs. The one on the far side of the table was occupied by a darkskinned, middle-aged woman who wore a very ordinary cotton dress and looked eminently respectable.

"Sit down," she said briskly in a voice that had a pronounced Cockney accent. "I don't use a crystal, nor the cards. Both your hands, please lady, the palms upward. That's the ticket."

Two rather small, beetle-black eyes gazed first at the outspread hands and then up into Arabel's face. "Well, goodness me, you have been mixed up with some queer doings," said Zillah, "and it's not all over yet, not by any means."


"I didn't know what to make of her," Arabel said, sitting opposite to Nicholas at a small table in the marquee. Most of the visitors had already had tea, and there was nobody to interrupt them. Prizes of the most tempting description were being bestowed on those competing in various games, and these contests attracted onlookers as well as competitors.

"Did she tell you anything that was remotely true?" Nicholas asked, a little anxious, because Arabel, who had been so gay and had looked so well at the beginning of the afternoon, was now pale and serious.

"I—well, I'm not sure. It *sounded* true when she said it, and she was so positive. She spent quite a long time looking at my hands—the palms—and comparing them with each other, and then she fixed me with her eyes, which are small and black and make one think of boot buttons, and said, "Now you listen serious, dear. You've got on to the right track, and you see you stay on it; no more of them drugs that's as good as rank poison to you, though more gradual. Nor any pills that may be given you, nor nothing else. She's not what she seems, that person what's so close to you, though I can't see as clearly as I'd like to and so can't tell you much about it. Jealousy, that's at the root of it, and always has been, but it looks as though she won't be with you much longer, and then you'll be out of danger. Don't you think hardly of your mother, lady, for her love for you was true. Mind yourself is the best advice I can give you. As for the men folk—well, they wish you well, though there's one who's as blindfolded as yourself.' . . ."

Arabel broke off, and Nicholas, who had been watching her closely said, "You've repeated that verbatim, haven't you? You have remembered every word of it."

"Well, yes. She impressed me, but then when she began to speak of the men who were in my life or would be, it all became rather absurd. I should marry and have a family, for although I might be warned against it, there was no reason why I shouldn't have sons and daughters, and there would be much opportunity to do good and to find happiness . . . oh, all that sort of thing, which one understands gypsies usually predict. It means nothing, but the other—about the drugs and danger . . ."

"What drugs and what danger?" demanded Nicholas, remembering all Charlotte's fears.

"I don't know, unless . . . Charlotte thought the tisanes my mrother brewed for me were harmful, and she persuaded me not to take them but to pretend I still was. Since I've given them up, I've felt completely different. I sleep soundly. I'm not nervous, and I have all the energy I need. It does seem to indicate that Charlotte's guess was right; those herbal potions don't suit me, though it goes without saying that my mother in urging me to take them had nothing but good intentions; besides, the gypsy expressly dwelt on her love for me—which naturally I have never doubted."

"Naturally." Nicholas agreed, resolved as he had been resolved all along, that Arabel should never, through an incautious word of his, suspect Charlotte's distrust of Mrs. Gibson.

"But then who does she mean by the person who is close to me, and it not what she seems to be? The only female person close to me at the moment is Charlotte, and it's absurd to suppose that she . . ."

"Oh, my dear girl, the whole thing is absurd."

"I might think so, only . . . how did she know I had been taking drugs and pills?"

"But have you? These soporifics probably contain nothing at all harmful." Yet even as he spoke, Nicholas uneasily remembered how he had been struck by the peculiarity of Arabel's eyes, the pupils mere pinpoints; and there had also been her occasionally confused manner. There were injurious ingredients which could be extracted from seemingly innocent wayside flowers, berries which were known to be poisonous, toadstools easily mistaken for mushrooms, but these were killers, and had Arabel been given them she would not be alive today. A town dweller, he knew next to nothing of country lore. Poppies contained opium, he thought hazily, and there was an evil purple blossom known as deadly nightshade. He recalled stories of old women who lived in hovels and who a generation ago were said to be witches. In those days they had been consulted by the lovelorn who paid heavily for love-potions.

"Better to be sleepless than to sleep by unnatural means," he said firmly. "Hot milk at night, with possibly a dash of brandy in it, is as much as I would prescribe."

"I don't need even that these days. Nicholas, you must admit it was an odd warning. What could the old woman have meant by jealously, and the person probably not being with me much longer?"

"It meant nothing. These people live by their wits and they pick up stray information by devious means and turn it to their advantage. Cosette believes in this creature and has probably chattered with her."

"But Mrs. Wentworth knows nothing whatever about me. I have only met her twice—once at your mother's dinner party, and the other day when she called at Troy Court."

"She has seen Charlotte more frequently, and Charlotte talks about you a good deal. Cosette wanted this party to be a success, wanted this fortune-teller to impress people. I wouldn't put it beyond her to supply her with snippets of gossip which she has twisted into portentous warnings. As you say yourself, these merged into the usual pattern about a future marriage. . . ."

"Well, there's certainly nobody who is likely to tell me I have no right to marry and have a family. Not that I'm in any hurry about either. I enjoy my freedom."

"Often that's another name for loneliness."

"I suppose it could be."

"And in loneliness one might turn to the wrong person. I wish, in that case, you could be persuaded to think of me as the right one."

Arabel did not doubt his sincerity. One way and another she had now seen a good deal of Nicholas Digby, and she valued the friendship that had sprung up between them. While lacking Kit's easy charm, there was much about him that appealed to her more than charm—for one thing, his respect for her intelligence and his sympathy with her wish to make full use of Troy Court, not only for herself but also for others. She gazed at him and thought he had the kindest face in the world; it was a clever face also, that of a mature man who had known much personal suffering and had also suffered from the pain of others that he had been unable to relieve. Irresistibly, comparing him with Kit, she was conscious of disloyalty, for Kit seemed immature beside Nicholas. But then wasn't she also immature, feeling as she did that she was moving through a dark forest, threatened by malign forces that must surely be imaginary?

She said, "I can imagine nobody to whom I would more readily turn if I were lonely."

"Or in any trouble?"

"Yes, of course . . . I'd be so grateful." She longed to tell him about Kit and the love that had sprung up between them, but loyalty held her silent, though she could not believe that Nicholas would think her wicked or unnatural. But he might justly think her shallow, since having had the sense of being spiritually torn in pieces, having known mingled despair and rapture, this already had a dreamlike unreality. She said involuntarily, "When I am with you, talking to you, I never feel that it's frustrating to be a woman."

"It's surely unnatural to feel that under any circumstances."

"Oh, I don't know, Nicholas, we have been suppressed for generations, and even now we have to fight for every inch, and men grudge us any independence."

"But you'll win, Arabel. As a sex you'll make mincemeat of us yet."

She laughed, "I don't know that I want as much as that, though I do want to be taken seriously. It must be heaven when love also means an intelligent companionship."

"My dear, haven't you understood that I long to give you both and to receive both in return?"

"How can you love me? You know so little about me."

"More than you think."

"Do you? I wonder." But she could believe that those keen, kind eyes did have the power to read beneath the surface and that he was possessed of an unusual understanding.

"You don't love me as yet, I know," he said, "but it occurred to me that it wouldn't be a bad idea to put the thought into your mind—where it may germinate." There was now a twinkling smile that invited her to join in a lighter mood.

"Oh, it will," she said. "Dear Nicholas, I like you so much. In fact I *like* you better than anyone else I know."

"That's a most encouraging start, especially as I like you—excessively."

"It could be almost more than love," she reflected.

"No, but combined with love, it's something to last forever. Don't worry, my dear, fate has a way of taking charge, and by that I don't mean the fate foreseen by any gypsy seeress. . . ."

He broke off. Charlotte had come into the marquee and was threading her way through the tables towards them. Hot, breathless, but evidently happy, she flung herself down into a chair and beamed at them both. "What a gorgeous party. I've played tennis, I've played croquet. I tried my hand at bowls and skittles and I've not won a single prize. Then, Madame Zillah being at liberty, after dozens had crawled in stealthily to consider her, I marched in boldly and unafraid, and she told me—"

"Things that were true," Arabel asked interestedly.

"No—unfortunately . . . she couldn't have been more wide of the mark. She thought I was one of a large family. Wherever did she get such an idea?"

"But—but you had told me your mother had had three babies who hadn't lived, before you arrived."

"Would they count?" Charlotte asked doubtfully.

"I don't know—perhaps."

Nicholas laughed. "As I've been telling Arabel, I'm convinced that Cosette has supplied considerable information," he said.

Arabel and Charlotte returned to Troy Court to find that Mrs. Gibson and Kit had also returned, but to their surprise they were told that Mrs. Gibson on arrival had gone straight to bed.

"But why?" asked Arabel. "Is she so tired? We're no later than we expected to be. We arranged that there should be a cold supper instead of dinner."

Kit was looking slightly perturbed. "Mother wasn't feeling well," he said. "In London it was very hot, and the train this evening was crowded. Some churl pushed her aside as she was getting in. She wasn't hurt, but it upset her—frightened her, I suppose. I noticed as I settled in her seat that she was looking a bad color —a leaden-gray color—and the train had barely started when she fainted. I had some difficulty in bringing her round, though fortunately I found a phial of *eau-de-Cologne* and some smelling salts in the handbag she took with her."

"I'd better go and see her," said Arabel in alarm.

"No, wait, Bel . . . I've just looked into her room and she was asleep. Better not disturb her for a while. It was nothing serious, I'm sure, for the odd thing is that while we were in London, while I was at my publishers', and Mother was supposed to be shopping in Regent Street, she was doing nothing of the kind. It appears she has had neuralgic headaches lately, and she decided on the spur of the minute, she says, to see a London doctor whom Lady Thora knew and consulted when they stayed in London. Fortunately she was able to make an appointment with him without previous notice. She says he gave her a thorough overhaul and assured her she was in perfectly good health physically, though she appeared to be under some strain, to have something on her mind. She did tell the doctor that she had been worried about you, Bel. . . ."

"But I've been so much better lately," Arabel protested. "And could just being worried make a person faint?"

"Hardly. It was the heat and the crush, and being roughly pushed, as I told you, but the medical examination must have been an ordeal, though I've no doubt the verdict was a relief. Mother says she has great faith in this man, though as you know, she has little faith in Galbraith."

Arabel agreed. Charlotte, feeling that this conversation was no business of hers, had tactfully left them together. "I'm sure she *has* been worried about me," Arabel said. "And about that wretched sleepwalking in particular. I'm thankful that . . ."

She broke off, for not even Kit must know that this had happened again.

"In many ways Mother has had a shockingly hard life," said Kit. "Comfortable, even luxurious, in one sense, but few things can be more exhausting than constant attendance on an invalid, especially as for years it meant conveying Lady Thora hither and thither in the hopeless quest for a cure. Then, too, there was the grief of being separated from you and from me, constantly putting our welfare first. I've never before realized this so keenly."

It was evident to Arabel that Kit was now suffering from a bad attack of remorse, with which she could sympathize, for hadn't she, of late, often felt remorseful about Ursula? She said, "But you have tried to make it up to her, Kit. The way in which you left the Heralds and came back to her has been such a joy to her, and now she has no need to worry anymore about me. I have never felt better."

Kit said reluctantly, "I hope she doesn't suspect that you—that we . . . you can't be sure with Mother. She keeps so much to herself."

"I'm certain it hasn't entered her head," said Arabel firmly. She hesitated and then braced herself to add, "In any case . . . dear Kit, this—this thing between us will right itself. I sometimes feel we have imagined half of it."

"What *do* you mean?"

"We were carried away, put up no resistance because it was so startling after years to meet again as grown-up strangers—for that is what we were, although so closely related. The child you had last seen was now—well, a pretty girl or at least pretty enough to pass; with money, fashionable clothes, everything to make her seem fascinating. As for me, I had always had a child's admiration for you and a longing to see you again, and when I did, and we met on equal terms, it was wonderful. I had never met anyone like you, so attractive, handsome and kind, on the way to fame. Was it any wonder we were both overthrown, for a time lost our balance?"

"Does this mean you have recovered your balance?"

"I think so, or at least I am on the way to recovering it."

"Arabel!" He stretched out his arm and drew her to him.

She did not draw away, she allowed him to kiss her, but her lips were cool. Kit gazed at her searchingly. She was lovely in her silver-gray dress, fragrant and sweet, but, if she was emotionally stirred by him, she was skillfully disguising it. Anger and chagrin stifled tenderness. He said, "I should have expected this. Unstable people are notoriously fickle."

She took this calmly. "Neither of us has behaved in a stable way. I sometimes find it hard to understand myself, or I should if I didn't realize that from the time I caught that chill I was in an extremely odd state and could scarcely distinguish between dreams and reality. I did try to explain to you."

"Yes," he was forced to admit. "Yes, you did."

The dreams she had described then had not seemed particularly portentous, but soon afterward Ursula's revelations had given it an ominous significance—the suggestion that at times Arabel suffered from delirious delusions. Now, Kit scarcely knew what to make of her, though the fear smote him that already her reason might be precariously balanced. Perhaps the unrest he had caused her had been too much for her, for it was beyond his understanding how a girl who had been so utterly in love a few days ago should now be able to dismiss this as a violent emotion which had burnt itself out.

Unhappy over Kit's chagrin, Arabel yet felt as though she had, with a supreme effort, wrenched apart fetters. She made an inadequate effort to justify herself. "It was as though I wasn't sane. If I had been I'd have put up a fight. I'd have been horrified and seen all the pitfalls before us. I know you've persuaded yourself that all we felt for each other was harmless, but it wasn't, Kit, or it wouldn't have been if I hadn't found the strength to pull myself together. Such love might have brought tragedy to us both."

Grudgingly he admitted it. "True enough, I dare say, though this cold shower of common sense has not yet descended upon me. Oh God, if only everything were different, if only there were no blood tie between us— although even then, marriage would have been too great a risk."

This puzzled her, but she said, "It's always a risk, surely."

"Yes—but with you . . ." Kit stopped on the brink of uttering words that could not have been easily explained, and for which he could not have forgiven himself. His anger with her had passed, though the disappointment and sense of loss remained. Retrieving, he said, "You're such a changeable girl that no man could ever feel sure of you."

"You can be sure of me in every other way. I shall

always be very, very fond of you, and I'm so proud of you."

"Well, that's something, I suppose—better than nothing." He turned away from her, more deeply wounded than he would have thought possible, though he supposed that he should welcome her change of heart. A vista of truly horrible possibilities rose up before him. He had been wearing blinkers. Thinking romantically of her tragic heritage, he had seen it as a barrier to her marriage with any man but never admitted that she could become violently deranged, an affliction not only to herself but also to her family.

This prospect was so appealing that it silenced him, and after a minute Arabel said, "I had better see if Ursula is awake. If so, I'll find out what she would like for supper. I *must* do everything I can to reassure her, to persuade her that she needn't worry about me any longer."

"What a kind, good girl you are," Ursula said affectionately. "Such a charmingly aranged tray. But you shouldn't have carried it up yourself, dear. Heaven knows, there are servants enough. . . ."

"Yes, of course there are. But haven't you sometimes felt you wanted to perform some little service for one you love?"

"Well, yes, naturally. Over and over again for Lady Thora, though I was in a position to give orders to any of the staff; and it has been the same for you too . . . the least little thing has given me pleasure—bringing you your tisane at nights, watching you drink it, seeing you settle down in drowsy comfort. But now that you have Charlotte here, that's all over. She follows at your heels like a puppy."

Arabel had already guessed that her mother was inclined to be jealous of Charlotte, and she was scarcely surprised at this, though she had not expected it to be so openly shown.

"She's certainly obsessively fond of you," Mrs. Gibson went on, "and she is so much a child that if one ventured to hint she was occasionally redundant she would probably burst into tears. How very appetizing this supper looks; cold salmon with a really colorful salad, and the pineapple mousse, which is one of the things Cook always manages successfully."

Arabel had provided a tray decoration in the shape of a rose in a slender glass, and Ursula now lifted this to her nose and sniffed at it delicately. "A really delightful touch," she approved.

Arabel was observing her attentively. Kit had said that before she fainted he had noticed her bad color, but her skin tones were normal enough now, though she might be slightly paler than usual.

"Kit was very worried about you," said Arabel, "and so was I when he told me. . . ."

"How foolish of you both. Didn't he explain that a lout on the platform at Waterloo nearly pushed me over?"

"Yes, it was disgraceful, but Kit thought you weren't hurt—and then you fainted."

"Naturally I should have disliked making an exhibition of myself at Waterloo, but I *was* somewhat hurt. The creature dug his elbow into my ribs and also trampled on my foot. He was wearing heavy boots. The pain was excessive, quite sufficient to cause fainting, though I did my best to fight it off."

It was ridiculous that Ursula should refer to this apologetically, thought Arabel. She said, "I can't think how you refrained from crying out, screaming . . . it's a pity you didn't, and then the horrible oaf would have realized. If there had been a policeman about he might even have been arrested."

"That wouldn't have been pleasant for any of us, would it?"

"No, but I feel furious when I think of it. Poor Ursula, you can't have had a pleasant day, visiting a doctor in London while Charlotte and I were having such fun at Cosette's garden party."

"I pictured you at it, my dear, and could imagine how charming you looked in your gray and lavender. I had no intention of consulting Dr. Parthen, but when Kit and I parted company, I had such neuralgia that I felt quite unfit for shopping. I have been troubled with it lately, and nothing I've taken has done it any good."

"Don't you know of a herbal cure for neuralgia?" Arabel asked with a glint of mischief in her eyes.

Mrs. Gibson smiled tolerably. "I do not, unfortunately. As for you, you never have believed in them, have you?"

"I don't think they did me any good, rather the reverse." And then, because this seemed as good a time as any in which to make confession, "Those tisanes for insomnia did make me sleep heavily for a few hours, but then I had the most horrid dreams and woke up, struggled awake as one does when one has a nightmare, and I felt dreadful—fearfully depressed and still in the nightmare although I was awake."

Ursula's gaze rested penetratingly upon her. "I gather," she said in a quiet voice, "that you are no longer taking the tisanes, though I have continued to bring you one each night. Why didn't you tell me?"

"I didn't want to be persuaded and I didn't want to hurt you. I haven't taken them for more than a week, and I'm sure you must have seen how much better I am."

"I certainly have, and with the utmost relief. You foolish girl, of course I am not hurt. Evidently, for some reason or other, you are the one person in a hundred to be adversely affected by a nature cure. I have prescribed the same mixture for others and it was of considerable help to them. Lady Thora took it from time to time when her rheumatic pains made sleep difficult. I am sorry you thought it necessary to deceive me."

"So am I, but it does seem sometimes as though one is impelled to deceive the people who mean the most to one. It's so painful to oppose them in any way."

"Well, yes, I see what you mean." Ursula patted Arabel's hand forgivingly. "But in this case the important thing is that your health is restored. Have you and Kit and Charlotte had supper, my dear?"

"Not yet."

"Then I expect you are all hungry. I am sure Kit must be, as he has eaten very little since luncheon, which we had together in London. A poor meal, though it was at the Apex Hotel, which is noted for its cuisine. The soup tasteless and the veal cutlets undone. I shall enjoy this delicious salmon."

"Shall I pour you a glass of wine before I leave you? Kit said the Chablis was excellent. He chose it for you himself."

Mrs. Gibson was pleased. "Dear boy, how thoughtful he always is. Do tell him, Arabel, that he need feel no anxiety about me."

"I will, of course, but he is sure to be up to see you after supper." Arabel stooped to kiss her mother's forehead and then departed.

Pleased though she usually was to receive any extra small attention from her son, Ursula Gibson was that evening thankful when he brought his visit to her to an end. She had never felt a more urgent desire to be alone, and although long steeled to self-control it was as much as she could do to repress her impatience when Arabel came in to see if there was anything further she required. With becoming gratitude for such concern, Ursula assured her there was not, and then at long last she was left in peace.

Determined to appear normal, she had eaten sufficient

of the salmon and salad and the pineapple mousse to satisfy Arabel, who had not only brought the tray but also had collected it. The wine had been welcome, though she would have preferred brandy. Fortunately she always kept a full flask of that in a small medicine cupboard, which, apart from the flask, contained only innocuous toilet waters and *eau-de-Cologne*. When she was sure there would be no further intrusions, she got out of bed and emptied half the contents of the flask into a medicine glass. This she swallowed without water and sighed with relief as the tingling warmth crept over her and the stimulant started to take effect.

It had been, she reflected, a dreadful day, and the way in which she had been hustled and trampled at Waterloo had been the least of it. Her one poor satisfaction was that neither Kit nor Arabel suspected anything, though it had been a blunder on her part to tell Kit that instead of shopping, she had spent a long session in Dr. Parthen's surgery and consulting room.

For that lapse of discretion her fainting fit was responsible. On recovering she had felt weak and ill, and when Kit had suggested stopping at Dr. Galbraith's house before driving on to Troy Court, it had seemed better to say truthfully that she had already consulted a doctor that day. But there truth had ended, for, far from being reassuring, Dr. Parthen had told her that her heart was in a precarious condition. Kind and cautious though he had been, Ursula divined that she had received, if not a death sentence, one that was not far removed from it. This she had accepted stoically, discounting what she judged to be no more than stereotyped reassurances. If she took very particular care of herself she might yet live for several years; but all exertion and agitation was to be avoided, and her family should be warned of her condition and of the attendant dangers.

Ursula had assured the kindly doctor that she would break this news in her own good time to her son and daughter. She would certainly avoid upsets, and, as for exertion, there was not the slightest need for it. She could be as idle as she chose. When Dr. Parthen suggested writing to her family doctor, she flatly forbade it and reminded him of the confidential bond between doctor and patient, which he was bound to respect. Paying her fee, she departed with her mind made up. Nobody should know that she was thus threatened.

Now, knowing it to be essential to her, she strove to control the furious anger that swept over her. She was still comparatively young and having always had good health had thought little of the occasional attacks of vertigo from which she had lately suffered; there had been pain also, however, and although she had put this down to a form of indigestion, it had been sufficiently severe to induce her to seek medical advice, not from the local doctor, of which she had a poor opinion, but from the eminent Dr. Parthen, of whom Lady Thora had thought highly.

Almost she could have wished that she had kept her illness a secret, even from a doctor, but if she had, she would have suffered considerable pain that could now be relieved. Dr. Parthen had given her a prescription for tablets, which she had, after leaving him, taken to the near chemist. These had been made up, and fortunately Kit had not noticed the small, sealed package when he had, in the train, ransacked her handbag for smelling salts.

Although she loved life and had contemplated a future which, when certain obstacles were overcome, she had expected to be luxurious and pleasurable, it was not now so much the probability that this could never be realized that tortured her, as concern for the one being she truly loved.

Even before Kit had discarded the Herald family, she had been determined that he should profit by her employer's death. For years she had dwelt upon this and had been divided between affection for Lady Thora

and the passionate desire to be in a position to give Kit
every conceivable luxury. She had been sure that the
greater part of Lady Thora's fortune would be hers;
there had been abundant hints to reassure her, and her
patience had been strained to the limit when the ailing
woman had lingered on for so many years.

When she had finally died, Ursula had genuinely
grieved, but not for long. Although she had been convinced that there was a later will than the one drawn up
over twenty years before, this was not in the solicitor's
possession and he knew nothing of its existence. For
Ursula there had been a few days of near despair until
she had discovered the sealed envelope addressed to Mr.
Brecknell, stating, in Lady Thora's writing, that it was
her last will and testament. It had of course been impossible for Ursula to break open the envelope and read
what was written within, but she had delivered it to the
solicitor with no misgivings. When she had been told
of the contents, she had been almost incredulous. From
her point of view, the one saving clause was that if
Arabel died before she was twenty-one, the entire fortune reverted to her, and contemplating this, her decision had soon been formed.

Those who knew Ursula Gibson and admired her
placid benevolence would, could they have seen her
now as she paced her room, have been sorely shocked,
for her handsome face was distorted by rage. The position had been bad enough before, and the time at her
disposal all too short, but now she could not be certain
of even a few months, far less of over a year. The sword
might fall upon her at any moment.

If only she dared to confide in Kit and to enlist his
help! But this she knew was impossible, so impossible
that her lips twisted in a wry smile. Kit, though he did
not know it, was her opponent, which was infuriating,
though in an obscure way it amused her. But for him,
Arabel might well have been dead by now and no further trouble to anyone. It was Kit, who stood to gain so

much by Arabel's death, who had saved her. She would, thought Ursula Gibson savagely, have broken her neck, falling down that long flight of stairs, but that Kit had leaped up to catch her. Recalling her own sensations on that memorable night, Ursula could only wonder that she had had sufficient presence of mind to conceal them.

She had consoled herself by the reflection that sooner or later she must be successful. The convolvulus seeds steeped and pounded that induced sleepwalking, hallucinations, and general mental confusion had had their expected effect, and, although Kit had rescued Arabel on one occasion, future draughts containing the drug would bring the girl to disaster.

It was maddening that Arabel was still safe. Who had put it into her head that the nightly tisanes were injurious? Ursula suspected the sharp-witted Charlotte. It was no secret to her that the girl disliked her. Ursula had been certain that Arabel would walk in her sleep again, and if she had locked the door as a precaution, what more natural than that being stifling, hot, and feverish, she should open the window, and meet the same fate as the Chinese bride of long ago?

A useful legend for Ursula's purpose, but although she had drawn back the bolts on the window, nothing had happened, though Arabel must have had some cause for alarm, since, as Ursula had lately discovered, a wire netting had been fixed outside the window. Had that precaution been taken on Charlotte's advice? Impossible to say, but if so, if the tiresome girl had her suspicions, she had evidently not confided them to Arabel, who when confessing a few hours ago that she had ceased to take the nightly tisane, had been innocently candid, and evidently only too thankful to be no longer deceiving her mother.

Now, unless Ursula could think of a better scheme, the convolvulus drug would have to be used in some other way, which presented difficulties, as there were so few occasions when Arabel, once more in good health and sharing all the family meals, took either food or drink that Kit and Charlotte did not also take.

One possibility after another flitted through Ursula's mind, but there was certainty in none of them. She could, she thought, contemplate her own death with resignation if Arabel went before her. Then, even though she might not be given time to make a will, Kit as her natural heir, would inherit Troy Court and all that went with it.

Her expression softened and her raging frustration dwindled as her thoughts dwelt on her son, and she recalled that moment of supreme happiness when he told her that he had thrown up all his prospects and had abandoned the Herald family for her sake. But she sighed and shook her head over his absurd optimism, his belief that as a novelist he could put himself beyond the reach of want. She had no such faith in a writing career, and invariably, when she thought of writers, poets, or artists, envisaged them starving miserably in garrets.

This should never happen to her adored Kit. She would risk anything to see him securely prosperous, but as yet she could leave him only a pittance. Arabel, certainly, might be generous and willing to help her half-brother, but it was all too likely that Kit in his independence would refuse to accept help.

If I die before her, Ursula mused, leaving my poor boy with such meager prospects, I shall be unable to rest peacefully in my grave.

This time her sense of macabre humor was not aroused, for it did not strike her as peculiar that a successful murderess should anticipate a peaceful oblivion.

Resentfully, impatiently, she became conscious of the uneven beating of her heart, of an accustomed dull heaviness which, although scarcely pain, was a danger signal. She had better, she supposed, take one of the pills that Dr. Parthen had prescribed, and finding the bottle still wrapped as delivered by the London chemist, she tore off the white paper, unscrewed the lid of the phial, and tipped a tablet into her palm.

So doing she recalled the doctor's instructions. The tablets, though lifesaving to one with her complaint, could be highly dangerous if taken by anyone else by mistake, and even to her, more than one tablet taken at stated times would be injurious. They should be kept safely in a locked drawer, Dr. Parthen had said. Ursula had promised to follow these instructions, but now having poured water into the glass that had contained the brandy and with its aid swallowed the tablet, she pondered. They were such small, harmless-looking pills. Suppose, just suppose, that by some mistake, some carelessness that would appear to have nothing to do with her, Arabel took a few of them? How many pills were likely to have a fatal result? How could she make sure of this?

# CHAPTER 10

Days passed, and to Ursula, conscious of the fate that threatened her, they passed with terrifying speed. The warm, sunny September was over, and with October there was the presage of winter—chilly mornings and evenings when fires were welcome. Arabel bought herself a fur cape, the first she had ever possessed; she stroked the soft sable with caressing fingers, scarcely able to believe that the costly wrap was hers. Ursula already had furs that Lady Thora had given her some weeks before her death, saying that she was convinced she would have no further use for them.

Already people were talking of Christmas and the traditional festivities. Charlotte supposed she would have to spend a few weeks in her own home, and, although for the actual Christmas holiday Arabel would be at Troy Court, she hoped she would join her afterward. Ursula could do nothing to prevent this, for Charlotte had spoken to Kit, saying how much she wanted Arabel to be her guest for a short while, which would hardly be possible if it meant leaving Mrs. Gibson alone for the beginning of the New Year. Good-naturedly, Kit had said that although he planned to settle into his Bloomsbury chambers during October, he would certainly return to Troy Court for Christmas, and would keep his mother company while Arabel was away. "Though it will be uncommonly quiet and dull without either of you," he concluded.

"Isn't it essential for a writer to be quiet and dull?" Charlotte inquired, and in her ingenuous eyes there was a flicker of coquetry.

"Not to that extent; in one's off hours one needs agreeable company, and your company is decidedly agreeable."

Charlotte colored with pleasure. "If that's true, I'm more than just conceitedly flattered. I'm proud in an—an uplifted kind of way."

Kit laughed and called her a goose, but being human he was gratified. When a few days later, advance copies of his first novel arrived, Charlotte received one, suitably autographed. Copies were also bestowed upon Mrs. Gibson and Arabel, but Charlotte had not expected such a gift and she was not only honored but also felt so extraordinarily happy that she was unable to hide it from Arabel.

"He's so wonderful," she said. "There can't be anyone in the whole world half so wonderful."

Arabel, who for a few, very few, weeks had thought the same, smiled sympathetically at the dreamy-eyed girl as she stood hugging the book to her breast. First love, since her own had changed so swiftly to an unexciting affection, was probably never very important; it was something you were almost bound to have, like mumps. All the same, mumps were unpleasant and painful, and she didn't want Charlotte to get hurt, which she would do since Kit had said not once but several times just lately that incestuous or not, unnatural or not, it would be an eternity before he could regard Arabel with the calm fondness to which her love for him had been transformed almost overnight. Every day now spent at Troy Court was a torment to him, and he would be thankful to remove himself to Bloomsbury. He would return for Christmas, because if he didn't his mother would be understandably upset, but he would have stayed only for the few indispensable days had not Arabel been leaving to stay with Charlotte.

As it was clear to Arabel that he was absolutely sincere, Kit was not a suitable person for Charlotte to expend her first love upon. He wouldn't even notice that she *was* in love with him since he was suffering in a fashion he angrily resented, and which made foolishness of the versifier's assertion that "It is half the world to me, dear, and all the world to you." Unaccountably, in the case of Kit and Arabel, this was reversed. When Arabel reminded him that it was her twentieth birthday in November and said that she would give a dinner party to celebrate it, for which she hoped he would be there, he said curtly that he doubted if he could manage it. He had undertaken to deliver the manuscript of his second book before Christmas, which would mean unremitting hard work. Writing, he told her crisply, was a dedication, and it was some slight balm to his fretted ego when Arabel said she had never doubted it, and that of course he mustn't give another thought to her unimportant birthday party.

His mother was less easy to pacify. In her way she was even more tormented than Kit. Although, when she had demanded of the doctor exactly how much longer she might be expected to live, and he had, according to his usual procedure in such cases, been vague, Mrs. Gibson realized that she would be optimistic indeed to believe in his comforting assurance that with care she might last for years; it was far more likely that she could only count on months or even weeks, and she yearned not to be parted from her son. Nor need she have been, had she told him the truth, for Kit's compassion and distress would have been greater than his urge to leave Troy Court. But this was her last intention. To be treated as an invalid would be more than she could endure, and besides, she would then be protectively watched, which would mean fewer opportunities for accomplishing that which she was determined to accomplish. Her one supreme desire was to outlive Arabel. When Arabel was dead, it would not matter how soon she followed, for she would leave Kit the owner of Troy Court.

Languor and pain were, however, making subtle inroads on Ursula's iron determination, and she was fretted because, in spite of her carefully detailed plans, nothing was working out smoothly. For Arabel, now in perfect health, it was useless to prepare any further nocturnal tisane, which she would refuse to take. And although Ursula still thought hopefully of the use to which her dangerous heart pills could be put, none of the medical books she consulted gave any information as to how many or how few might be lethal. If Arabel had taken her breakfast in bed, it might have been possible to experiment, to slip a few tablets into the teapot, which would have been emptied, washed, and set on its usual shelf before the poison took effect. But Arabel rose for breakfast each morning, and Mrs. Gibson had discovered that as often as not she did not touch the morning tea that Bessie left beside her bed.

Even had this method been possible, it was not a really satisfactory one. Ursula could not overlook the fact that a sudden, inexplicable death might mean a postmortem, and when it was discovered that Arabel had been poisoned, there would be investigations, and a general suspicion of foul play, for who could suppose that a healthy, beautiful girl, heiress to a large fortune, would, unless there was some reason for it, take her own life?

But of course there *was* a reason, though Arabel was unaware of it. At the back of Ursula Gibson's mind there had always been the thought that one day it might be useful to enlighten her. Then—surely—it would not be so extraordinary, if suddenly discovering that on her father's side there was the taint of madness, she was sufficiently horrified to feel that life was unbearable.

Who, however, *could* enlighten Arabel when nobody knew of this tragic heritage except Ursula and Kit? She would have to find out in a more devious manner Ursula decided, and she was still exasperatingly puzzling over this when the opportunity presented itself.

One afternoon she walked into the library to find Arabel curled up on the window seat fast asleep with a book on her knee. For a few seconds Mrs. Gibson surveyed her in a curiously dispassionate fashion, remembering how Arabel had said somewhat scornfully that it was only old people and invalids who needed rest in the afternoons, and it was true that she was generally energetic. And Mrs. Gibson glanced at the fire that was far too large for a mild day; the heat of the room must have overcome her; also, she had been out most of the morning in Nicholas Digby's dogcart—not as a passenger but driving under his instructions. Returning to Troy Court for luncheon, she had been gay, exhilarated, with a fine color in her cheeks, but she had yawned too, and had said the cold air and the speed at which the horse had taken them had made her feel sleepy.

As Mrs. Gibson stood watching Arabel, two things happened—the girl's eyelids quivered as though she was on the verge of waking, and Kit came in with two or three heavy books under his arm. His mother saw a flashing possibility. "Just look at her," she said indulgently. "She's sleeping like a child."

Kit came to his mother's side. He observed Arabel in her relaxed loveliness with a pain and regret that Ursula was far from suspecting.

"There are times when her likeness to her poor father is almost uncanny," said Ursula. "This is one of them. He too looked so young and defenseless when asleep. Nicholas Digby with his driving lessons must have tired her out this morning. I'm getting worried about that association. He's quite openly devoted, and although nobody could call Arabel forward, she does seem to encourage him. I feel responsible. It would be cruel to them both to let things go too far—while Arabel is in ignorance, I mean."

"Don't speak of it now—you may waken her," Kit said.

Ursula, who suspected that Arabel was on the verge of waking, said confidently, "Oh no, she's deeply asleep, poor child. Sometimes I feel quite heartbroken when I consider all that threatens her."

"It may never be more than a threat, Mother."

"I wish I could believe that, but unfortunately, remembering her father, I recognize the ominous signs, and as this curse has been transmitted through the generations, how can one hope that poor Arabel will escape?"

"Escape what?" Arabel's eyes were wide open. She raised herself to a sitting position, and Mrs. Gibson uttered a sharp exclamation.

"Nothing," said Kit, "we were talking at random . . . just nonsense, and you were more than half-asleep . . . what I mean is that we were discussing a hypothetical case." His words, utterly unconvincing, tumbled over one another.

Arabel's gaze turned from him to her silent mother. She said, "None of that is true, I'm afraid. You were talking about *me*. I heard enough to be sure of it. What did you mean, Ursula, by ominous signs and a curse that has been transmitted through my father?"

"Oh, my poor, dear child!" Mrs. Gibson turned away with a stifled sob.

"Bel, I do assure you it was nothing of any importance," Kit said desperately. "Let it drop. . . ."

"How can I? It's not possible. I overheard too much, and even if you both refuse to explain, it will haunt me, and sooner or later I shall puzzle it out for myself. Besides, if I'm threatened with some hereditary illness, surely I have the right to know about it. It is that, isn't it? It explains why Ursula has worried so much about my health."

"There's nothing wrong with your health, dear, I swear it. Can't you trust me?" Kit pleaded with deep distress.

"No, I cannot, and with good reason. You know very well that for some reason or other you are bent on deceiving me. Ursula—please. . . ."

Mrs. Gibson put a hand to her heart as a sharp pain pierced her. She sat down in the nearest chair, and her other hand went up to cover her face. She said in a stifled voice, "I *must* tell her, Kit. I have always known that one day I should have to tell her, and as she says, she has the right to know."

"But . . . oh God, it's too cruel!" Kit exclaimed. Arabel was on her feet now but he drew her down to the window seat again and put his arm round her. "Dear, dearest Bel, it may never happen. I think, myself, that Mother takes too gloomy a view."

Arabel's body was rigid within his encircling arm; she was very pale. "I can judge that for myself when I know what it is that threatens me. What was wrong with my father? I was told that he died, while at sea, of a tropical fever. Wasn't that true?"

Mrs. Gibson said defensively, "When you first started to ask questions, you were only a child, and it was impossible to tell you the truth."

"Yes—well, I am no longer a child." Tension expressed itself in impatience. "Whatever the mystery, you can't hide it from me now."

Mrs. Gibson shook her head as though struck to speechlessness and it was Kit who said, "Your father's death did occur when he was in the tropics, and such intense heat has before now overset a man's reason."

"It's useless to try to put me off with half-truths, Kit. How *did* he die?" Arabel demanded.

Ursula told her.

Arabel stole out of the Chinese room. After an impassioned argument with Kit, she had been left alone there.

"I shall go out of my mind here and now," she had cried, "unless I can be by myself. Yes, of course, this has been a ghastly shock, but I shall get over it if I'm given the chance. The one thing I can't bear now is to be watched, pitied, treated as though I'm already a lunatic."

Finally Ursula had persuaded Kit to give way to her. Arabel had run up the stairs and locked herself into her room. But she had no intention of staying there; she craved to be out in the open. Presently, when she thought it unlikely she would be heard, for Kit was shut away in the library and Mrs. Gibson had said exhaustedly that she had intended to lie down, she threw on a cape with an attached hood, changed her slippers to walking shoes, and went softly down the stairs. As noiselessly as possible she let herself out of the house, thankful that Charlotte was spending the day with Cosette Wentworth at the Tower House.

The afternoon, drawing towards its close, was chilly; the sky was overcast after a fine morning, and it looked as though it might rain at any moment, but to Arabel in her present state of mind, such weather was preferable to sunshine. She was not stunned by her mother's revelation, and thought now that for weeks and months she had been anticipating some shattering blow. At last everything added up—the incautious, little-understood words that Kit had dropped from time to time when under the stress of emotion; her mother's exaggerated solicitude; and indeed her own violent changes of mood.

It seemed to her now that no sanely balanced young woman could have conceived such a sudden, wild infatuation for her half-brother and as suddenly recovered from it. How feeble, how utterly unconvincing, to have told herself that this was because first love was not the kind of love that could be expected to last, especially when by the laws of consanguinity it was disgraceful, iniquitous to have fallen in love with Kit in the first place. She had known it was madness, and so it was—such madness as might be expected of her father's daughter, and the more deplorable because it had all seemed so natural, so right to love and be loved in return. She had constantly had to remind herself of the relationship and the boredom of such reminders might possibly account for the short duration of her infatuation. But no . . . it was because she was unstable. Oh heaven, what would become of her! She might develop into one of those unspeakable women who pursued men with their unwanted love.

Although it was impossible for Arabel to blame her mother, who had naturally wanted to hide this terrible thing from her for as long as it was possible to hide it, she did feel that demanding the truth today and receiving it with undoubted anguish on Kit's part, her mother might have been less pessimistic, might have refrained from pointing out that the extreme obstinacy she had shown lately was an ominous sign. Kit had derided this, but Ursula Gibson's words had sunk deep into Arabel's consciousness. She was so reckless, so resolved to have her own headstrong way however unsuitable, accused Ursula. Charlotte's presence, for instance, at Troy Court, which for such a long period was an embarrassment, and took a good deal of explaining to people, who naturally thought Charlotte's parents were paying them. What could be more disagreeable. Though, indeed, this was a small matter compared with the crazy notions of turning Troy Court into a home for needy invalids. . . .

There had been a good deal of this, which was unusual, for Ursula was no nagger, and to Arabel it seemed inhuman and cruel that on this terrible day she should have been so reproached. Now as she walked swiftly over the fields, thankful to be putting a distance between herself and Troy Court, the memory of her mother's face as she had delivered these denunciations flashed through her distracted mind, and it could have been the face of a stranger. Ursula, she realized, though at the time she had been in no state to realize it, had looked wretchedly ill, her skin heavily pallid, her eyes dull; the peculiar cruelty of pointing out to her horrified daughter that she was already showing signs of dementia could be excused because she too was suffering from a species of shock—emotionally torn in pieces, poor thing, thought Arabel pityingly.

Although Ursula must have known that finally she would have to tell her daughter the truth, if indeed Arabel was not already raving mad before she summoned up sufficient resolution, she had certainly not intended to tell her today, without preparation, and she must have been thoroughly upset because her conversation with Kit had been overheard. But it didn't really matter that she knew about herself at last, Arabel thought. The thing of consequence was that not only her father but also his mother before him, and perhaps more remote ancestors, had been violently insane.

Poor Kit had endeavored to reassure her, to water down the truth, but it was no good. Arabel had questioned her mother and had insisted on receiving bald and truthful answers. From the hour of her daughter's birth, Ursula confessed, she had dreaded this hour, though while Arabel was at Seacrest living a quiet, disciplined life, she had been able to stifle her fears. It had needed no further words to outline her future, which at the best must be dark with fear, even if by the mercy of heaven she escaped a worse fate.

Arabel's confused mental ramblings had kept pace with her swift footsteps, although these were impeded by her long, full skirts. Once she stepped on the hem and barely escaped being thrown headlong; and then when she came to a stile, she had to bunch her clothes around her in order to climb over it. As she had walked, sometimes indeed half-running for a considerable distance, she was weary enough to sit down on the topmost step, and there, overcome by fatigue and wretchedness, forgetful that she was now facing the highway, she covered her face with her hands and not only shed tears but also broke into loud, gulping sobs. Both were a relief to her overcharged heart, and she had no thought to spare for the woeful figure she would present to any passerby, until a hand touched her shoulder. "What for pity's sake is wrong? My dear girl, are you ill? Have you hurt yourself?"

She shook her head on a gasp of relief and uttered brokenly, "Oh, if anyone had to find me—to see me—like this, how thankful I am it is you."

"Well, yes, so am I," said Nicholas. He produced a large white handkerchief, unfolded it and handed it to Arabel.

She dabbed at her streaming eyes and said, "You must think I'm mad, sitting here, crying out loud, and if you do think so, you will be right, for that's just what I am . . . mad—mad—mad!"

Suppressing his consternation he retorted, "Even if you are, my love, you won't achieve sanity by hysterics. Get up now, it's starting to rain and then you'll be in even worse case. I'll take you home—to my home, not yours; we're within a few hundred yards of it, you know."

"Green Lawns? I hadn't any idea where I was. I've been walking blindly across the fields. But I can't let your mother see me looking like this—terrible."

"My father and mother are both out and won't be home for an hour or more. By then you will have washed your face and had tea and will have told me the gist, at least, of what is wrong. You'll be feeling considerably better. It's a lucky thing that I took the dogs for a walk and found you here. Where have they got to, I wonder?"

He raised his voice and called, and the two spaniels came lumbering through the grass towards him. Nicholas lifted Arabel from the stile, and careless of whom they might meet on the way to Green Lawns, tucked her hand into his arm. Arriving at his home, he handed her over to a kindly, middle-aged maid with the mendacious statement that walking across the fields Miss Gibson had stumbled and wrenched her foot. It had caused her pain, and when he had fortunately come upon her by chance, she was in tears, wondering how she would get back to Troy Court. However, all she now needed was a rest and some tea, and no doubt she would be glad of warm water to wash her tearstains away.

The sympathetic maid bore Arabel away to a bedroom, removed her cape saying she would give it a brush, necessary enough since in her heedless rambling Arabel had plunged through bushes which had scattered their falling leaves on her, and supplied her not only with hot water, towel and soap but also with a brush and comb.

Within five minutes Arabel was feeling composed and greatly refreshed. She was looking much as usual when she joined Nicholas in the drawing room, where there was a cheerful fire and tea waiting. Pouring out tea for them both, eating hot, buttered scones helped to steady her, but later, when the tea tray had been removed, it took all her self-control to tell Nicholas what she had only recently discovered about her father and his mother before him. They sat on the sofa drawn up before the fire, and her story was not half-told before his arm was around her and her head resting on his shoulder.

Arabel kept nothing from him. He heard not only all that her mother had related; but also about her brief, tumultuous love for Kit, which had so soon become no more than a natural warm affection. "It does seem as though only an unbalanced person would have felt anything else," Arabel said, once more near to tears. "And there's so much besides—my nightmares and sleepwalking, though I do think, as you know, that they were at least aggravated by the herbal tisanes my mother persuaded me to take."

"None of this adds up to anything of much significance," Nicholas said. "You are not unbalanced in any particular, my dear, far less on the way to insanity. Also, has it not occurred to you that you have no real proof that your father was out of his mind? Nor has Mrs. Gibson."

"But—but to kill himself as he did . . . and then, too, his strange moods, which frightened her so much—and what he told her about my grandmother."

"Arabel, we don't know what state he was in, poor fellow, when he threw himself overboard. He may well have been suffering from madness but from some tropical illness which caused a delirium. As for the depression and changes of moods that alarmed Mrs. Gibson, would not they be almost inevitable if he had an obsession that he was going the same way as his mother? Though there is not, as you will realize if you think calmly, the slightest evidence of what caused his mother's dementia. She could have met with some accident, it could have been the result of some altogether different illness; she may have suffered in some terrible way that threw her off balance. Your father, so far as I can gather, only told Mrs. Gibson the bare facts."

"Yes, that is true, but . . . all the same it's a dreadful heritage, Nicholas."

"Certainly not a happy one, my love; but I do not believe for a moment that you are threatened with the same fate. You have gone through an upheaval in more senses than one and have emerged intact."

"But don't you think it was—was extraordinary that I should have fallen in and out of love with Kit, all within the space of a few weeks? And he—he is my half-brother, though even now I can't make myself feel as though he is."

"Well, no," said Nicholas with a placidity which in itself was balm. "It doesn't strike me as being so singular. People do get carried away by these sudden attractions; it's a superficial thing, and naturally doesn't last. I don't, of course, know how it is with Kit Herald—maybe it went deeper; but he's an attractive fellow, clever, pleasant-mannered, and the type to whom most women are drawn, I should imagine. Not having met many men, and as you say, with nothing to remind you of the relationship, you forgot it for a while—mistook fascination for love—but would have found out your mistake and retracted, I believe, even had there been no relationship. He isn't the right man for you, my dear, but I am. . . ."

"Nicholas, how can you think . . . ?"

"All I think is that you need someone older, far less physically attractive, but perhaps more dependable, than Herald; someone who understands you better and loves you deeply, someone who if the moon and the stars were his would give them to you as playthings. But as it is, I can give you nothing spectacular. I've been ill and my career has come to a temporary standstill. But it *is* only temporary. I have a reasonable private income—which is no match for yours, but then I don't happen to think of money as a barrier. It's something to be used as wisely as possible, not wholly for one's own aggrandizement. You—broadly speaking—feel the same, I know."

"Yes . . . yes, I do, but . . . I don't understand . . . how *can* you think I am marriageable after all I have told you? It would be a terrible risk."

"A very slight risk, perhaps," Nicholas admitted, "though I'm not even sure it is that. As I've said, I doubt if anyone knows the entire truth or ever will know it, but I'm convinced beyond all argument that you are as sane as I am—or saner—and that you will remain so."

He saw the strain fade slowly from her face, felt her relax within his encircling arm. "But suppose you are wrong?" she said fearfully.

"That's where the very slight risk comes in—to me it

is infinitesimal. But if it will ease your mind, I'll take you along to see a friend of mine in London who specializes in mental illnesses. Doctors know far too little about the processes of the mind, but they do know something, and there *are* tests. I haven't the least doubt that you would pass them with ease, and that my friend would give us his blessing and wish us joy."

"Oh how happy you've made me," Arabel uttered, "and I thought I could never be happy again."

"That's the most important thing in the world to me —that and the hope of winning your love."

"Nicholas," said Arabel solemnly, "at the moment I feel as though I adore you as never man was adored before."

He broke into laughter, and after a few seconds she also laughed. "But it's true," she protested.

"My sweet, I don't doubt it. I've no doubt that a transport of adoration is lavished on firemen who rescue terrified victims from burning houses, but I'm not seeking that particular brand of adoration. No need to rush things. Almost from the first I had this certainty that sooner or later we should belong to each other—though I dare say that sounds arrogant."

"No, it doesn't, because you're not an arrogant person. There *are* times when one is absolutely positive about something, though one can't say exactly why. It has happened to me once or twice. I think the most vivid was when I was only a child and was leaving Troy Court for the first time to go to Seacrest. I was terribly miserable about it. I couldn't imagine how I was going to bear it, and my mother seemed so calm and indifferent because I was going away. I know now that she wasn't but was only pretending, thinking that if she showed she was miserable it would make it worse for me; but of course a child of twelve couldn't be expected to understand that."

"No, she couldn't," Nicholas agreed, studying her expression, pitying that lonely child of years ago.

"Almost at the last," Arabel went on, "I was sent to Lady Thora in her room to say good-bye to her. I expect she had asked to see me. My mother was called away by someone while Lady Thora was still talking to me. We were alone, and I can't remember that we had ever been left alone together before, though I suppose that must have happened occasionally. I was standing beside Lady Thora, who was half-sitting, half-lying on the chaise longue, and I thought—it came over me suddenly in a wave—how sweet and kind she was, and pretty too, although she was nearly always ill. She seemed so much a part of Troy Court; she belonged to it, and in the oddest way I was sure I belonged to it too, and she said, 'You love this old place, don't you, Arabel?' I told her I did, that to me it was the most beautiful house in the world, and that I wished I need never leave it. I was conscious that she watched me as though she couldn't take her eyes from my face. She said, 'Ursula's right, no doubt, but I wish you needn't leave here, or leave me.' There were tears in her eyes, and I had been crying all the morning. She drew me down to her and kissed me and said, 'Remember I love you. You must think of me, and I shall think of you, and if there's anything you want—especially—you must ask me for it . . . nobody has a better right.' Ursula came in then, and we could say nothing more, for she was vexed because Lady Thora looked distressed and said I should have known better than to upset her. She hustled me off, and it was months before I saw Lady Thora again. I am sure now that it was when I said I loved Troy Court so much that the inspiration came to her to leave it to me, to make me her heiress. It was— it was a moment of truth. When she said that nobody had a better right, she was already thinking of me as the one who would come after her."

"Yes—she probably was," Nicholas agreed. He had listened attentively, as he had listened to all Arabel had told him within the last hour. He was conscious of confusion, of much to be sorted out, of various implications in her story that at present eluded him. He drew her close to him and said, "I meant it when I told you there was no need to rush things, but tell me one thing. Have you the same belief, the same confidence, that we shall marry and be happy?"

"Yes, yes, I have." She put her hand into his, and a blissful peace took possession of her.

"Then I think," said Nicholas, though he was not absolutely certain why this seemed so important, "that as soon as possible you should tell your mother. We have not known each other very long and need not tell anyone just yet that we are engaged, but she should certainly know."

"She won't approve. She will think it wrong, Nicholas."

"Never mind that. I'm prepared to answer all her arguments. You must tell her, though, that I know everything; that I love you and have no fear for the future. Will you do that, Arabel?"

"Yes, I will."

"And be sure to impress on her that you are happy to belong to me," Nicholas said.

# CHAPTER 11

Nicholas, having no clear idea of why he had impressed on Arabel that at the earliest opportunity Mrs. Gibson should be told of their engagement, pondered over it after she had been sent home in the Digby's landau with a maid to accompany her, for Mrs. Digby had considered it highly improper for Nicholas to escort her.

Since he had not shared Charlotte's distrust of Mrs. Gibson, it now seemed odd, to say the least, that he was conscious of a profound uneasiness when he considered her. Their encounters had been slight, but he had thought her a more than usually pleasant woman who, if anything, was so attached to her daughter that she worried unnecessarily about her.

Arabel, in relating her story, had said nothing against her mother, had not referred to the way in which she had been reproached for her intransigence at the crucial hour when she had stood most in need of tender pity. That, she thought, was between Ursula and herself, but Nicholas had divined a lack of sympathy.

Now, late in the evening, recalling all Arabel had told him, he started to fit minute pieces together, which eventually formed a mosaic. The pattern was imperfect, but even so it was sufficiently alarming, for he had come to the conclusion that Charlotte, young though she was, had been more clear-sighted than himself. Ursula Gibson was not the simple, kindly person she appeared to be.

Arabel, in briefly alluding to the life that her mother had mapped out for her before Lady Thora's death, had said with evident belief that such plans had been in her own best interests, but Nicholas now found it hard to credit this. There had been so much affection between Lady Thora and Arabel that it had surely been unnecessary to insist on such a drastic separation. Arabel could at least have been sent to a school near Troy Court where the invalid might have seen more of her during her childhood, for Lady Thora had not traveled extensively until the last two years of her life. It was a disturbing thought that Mrs. Gibson had made no effort to visit her daughter at Seacrest College and had seldom written to her. It was only after Lady Thora's death, when Arabel was known to be her heiress, that she had returned to Troy Court.

Incidents since then, though when they were taken separately they could be viewed as trivial, were less so when viewed as a whole. There were not only the herbal tisanes, which might or might not be injurious, but also the danger of Arabel's sleepwalking, and the window that should have been securely bolted but was not.

The way in which Arabel had discovered the truth about her father seemed to Nicholas to be contrived, unnatural. How in the world could Ursula Gibson have been certain that she was soundly asleep? A brief after-luncheon nap following a morning spent in the open air learning how to drive a mettlesome horse would more likely be a light doze, from which one partially unconscious would easily be aroused. How then did it come about that Mrs. Gibson had started this conversation with Kit, not in a subdued murmur but speaking so loudly that the girl was inevitably wakened? Did this indicate that Ursula Gibson planned she should hear what was being said? Had it become imperative that she should ask questions, to be told the brutal truth? If so—why?

When Charlotte had told him that if Arabel died her mother would inherit Troy Court, he had seen no significance in it. It was heinous to suppose a girl's mother could wish her to die, yet he was now more than half-inclined to believe that this was exactly what Ursula did wish, and in persuading Arabel to promise that she would tell her mother all, he had obeyed an unanalyzed instinct. Some sixth sense had warned him of danger, which might be less if Mrs. Gibson knew that Arabel was under his protection, that she was happy, and that harm to her could not be explained by the fact that she was distractedly worried over her parentage.

By the time Nicholas had sorted this out he was in such a state of anxiety that he would, had it been possible, have gone straight away to Troy Court, demanding to see Arabel. But it was past midnight and he could do nothing. Even when he next saw the girl, how could he suggest anything drastic, urge her to leave Troy Court immediately? His suspicions were melodramatic, and Arabel would not believe what he himself did not wholly believe.

The long hours before daylight stretched endlessly before him. They were torturing hours—not the less so because he was more than half-persuaded that in the calm light of day his fears would seem ridiculous.


At Troy Court after dinner that evening, there occurred a slight, but definitely unpleasant, scene. Mrs. Gibson had discovered, through an incautious remark dropped by Bessie, the head housemaid, that Charlotte was not sleeping in her own room. With a solicitude that barely concealed disapproval, she inquired why. Was Charlotte not content with Lady Thora's suite? This, said Ursula, was the most spacious and pleasant in the entire wing, and she herself had personally seen that their young guest had everything she required.

"I feel rather lonely sometimes," Charlotte said, "and Arabel doesn't mind sharing her big bed with me."

"Nevertheless, my dear, it is not suitable," Ursula pronounced, "and really not at all fair to Arabel, who sleeps so badly."

"Not now," Arabel said. "As I told you, I have been sleeping soundly these nights, and Charlotte is no longer keeping me company."

"I fancy," said Ursula, "that it is you, my dear, not Charlotte, who is nervous of sleeping alone, in which case I will have my bed moved into your room. Then you can dispense with that rather unsightly wire netting outside your window, which I have only recently noticed. Why did you not tell me that you were apprehensive of sleepwalking again? Have you had any further trouble in that way?"

"No . . . I . . . well, I did wake up one night to find that I was standing by the window." Arabel, who, as she had said, was not adept at telling lies, ignored Charlotte's scowl and produced this half-truth.

"Oh, dear! Oh, my child, why didn't you tell me? No—please don't say that you were silent because you were unwilling to worry me. It is far more worrying to feel that I am being deceived, kept in the dark. If you have any such symptoms it is my right to know."

"Symptoms of what?" Charlotte had the temerity to ask.

Mrs. Gibson gazed at her with an abstracted expression. "You wouldn't understand."

"It isn't such an extraordinary thing to walk in one's sleep," Charlotte persisted. "I know Arabel did do this once and would have fallen down the stairs if Kit had not caught her. But we talked it over and were quite sure that this only happened because she was taking a nighttime drink that disturbed her mind instead of soothing it."

"Really! I had no idea that you were so much in my daughter's confidence."

"But why shouldn't I be?"

Kit, who had been lingering at the dinner table over a glass of port and a cigar, came into the drawing room and caught the last words. Aware of tension, he glanced from his mother's stony face to Charlotte's flushed one.

"Because," said Mrs. Gibson, "this . . . er . . . peculiarity of Arabel's is a family matter and causes us some concern. It has nothing whatever to do with the herbal tisanes I recommended her to take, and if she has discussed the matter with you, I can only say that I strongly disapprove. You are here, not only as a guest but also as a pupil, and should be protected from—er —unpleasantness, not have it forced upon you by Arabel, who at Seacrest was in authority over you."

"Not really, Mrs. Gibson. Pupil teachers have no authority—they are a . . . a sort of hybrid. Arabel was not much above the level of a senior girl and we were friends."

"What *is* all this?" Kit asked, dropping down into a chair drawn close to Arabel.

"Nothing," she replied, "or nothing of importance."

"Knowing what you—unfortunately—have forced me to reveal today, I wonder you can say so," Mrs. Gibson retorted. "Surely you can see for yourself that it is not right for Charlotte to be here. I have never approved of the arrangement, and with good reason, as any normally responsible person would agree. I am your guardian, Arabel, and for the next year at least my wishes should be respected. Either you will write to Charlotte's parents, telling them it is inconvenient for her to return after the Christmas holiday, or I shall be forced to do so."

Charlotte stared at her in amazed indignation.

"But what have I done?" she demanded.

"Nothing, my dear." Mrs. Gibson spoke more mildly. "But there are reasons that do not concern you."

"But they *do* concern me. It's as though I am being sent away in disgrace."

"Charlotte, that is nonsense," Kit expostulated.

"It isn't nonsense. Is it a crime that I am fond of Arabel, and that she is fond of me?"

"Certainly not, but . . ."

"Do *you* want to send me home, Kit?" There were tears in Charlotte's eyes, and he was touched by this supplication. He also realized that he would miss her—miss her admiration and her vivid interest in his writing, which made her a stimulating companion.

"Of course I don't want you to leave," he said, "but I can see my mother's point of view. She has been worried about Arabel for a long time, thinks her unfit for the responsibility. . . ."

"I don't believe it," Charlotte cried, and rising, she fixed Mrs. Gibson with hostile eyes. "To me it seems quite clear that your mother dislikes me because she is jealous."

"I don't dislike you, Charlotte," said Mrs. Gibson kindly. "But I have thought all along that the arrangement Arabel made with you lacked dignity . . . for her, taking into consideration the great change in her position. It was completely different when it was necessary for her to teach at Seacrest."

"That does seem to me to be the most despicable snobbery," retorted Charlotte hotly, and then she turned, and with a great swaying and flouncing of her crinoline went out of the room. If she did not exactly slam the door behind her, she certainly closed it with a sharpness that caused several ornaments to shiver.


"The girl was insolent," said Ursula Gibson, "but there is no necessity for you to upset yourself about it, my dear. Of course you had to go after her. One would not wish the silly child to be in floods of tears and uncomforted."

"Charlotte wasn't in floods of tears," Arabel smiled slightly. "When I went to her sitting room she was working on her French translation and was perfectly calm. You seem to be more upset than she is, and I wanted to be alone with you, to have—well, to have a talk with you."

"Then sit down, Arabel; we may as well be comfortable. I have no doubt there are many questions that have occurred to you, and I will certainly answer them. It has been a painfully upsetting day for you, I know, and I only wish it had not been necessary to tell you about your poor father."

"That could not have been concealed forever."

"No, but I do beg you to keep this matter to yourself —not to confide in Charlotte. For one thing, she is too young to be burdened with such a tragic story, and for another, she would be sure to tell her mother, who in her turn would probably repeat it to others. It is not the kind of story one would wish to have circulated far and wide. But try not to be too upset. If you live quietly, placidly, all may yet be well."

To this Arabel made no immediate reply, and Mrs. Gibson said with a semblance of cheerfulness, "Come now, take courage. In a few days you will have recovered from the shock, and nothing will seem so bad. I wonder if a glass of champagne would help. Kit, the dear boy, had heard me say that there were still several bottles of a stock that Lord Riba laid down several years ago. He suggested that a few bottles should be brought up from the cellar and insisted that I had one in my own room. He thought champagne might help my neuralgia."

"The only time I tasted champagne was at Green Lawns, when we dined there. I thought it not very different from cider."

Mrs. Gibson laughed quite gaily. "Did you really? But it has an exhilarating effect which all other wines lack." She rose, went to her bureau, produced a bottle, and then exclaimed with vexation, "Oh dear, of course there *is* only the one glass. But I'll ring for a maid to fetch another."

"They'll all be at supper," Arabel said. "I'll get one from the dining room."

"That's considerate of you, dear."

How easily, how naturally, the girl had fallen into the trap. Mrs. Gibson beamed at her, and once Arabel had gone out of the room she lost no time, but went quickly to her medicine cupboard and took from it the box of pills marked DANGEROUS. It was a pity she hadn't yet discovered how many pills would be fatally dangerous, but five or six should surely be sufficient to bring about serious illness, if not death itself, and once Arabel was in a helpless state, the dose could be repeated. The cause of death would no doubt be discovered, but who could possibly blame Arabel's mother? Without a doubt the girl herself would be held responsible. Kit knew that she was in a distraught state of mind and there was sufficient reason for it. This he would testify, and the worst that could be said of Mrs. Gibson was that she had been careless to leave the medicine cupboard unlocked, thus giving her daughter, in dread of future insanity, the means and the opportunity to destroy herself.

By the time Arabel returned, one glass of wine was already poured out, and Mrs. Gibson put it into her hand. She took the other glass and filled it. Arabel looked at the golden liquid thoughtfully. She said. "It's an appropriate occasion for champagne."

"Certainly it is; one needs a stimulant occasionally."

"Yes, but there's a particular reason for celebration. This afternoon I went for a long walk. I couldn't bear it in the house, just pacing up and down the Chinese room in a state of terror. I walked and walked. In a circle part of the time, for I didn't notice where I was going. At last, when I was really worn out, I sat down on a stile, and I cried, and Nicholas found me there. He was giving his dogs a run and he took me to Green Lawns."

Ursula was gazing at her with consternation, "Oh, Arabel, for heaven's sake! You surely didn't tell the Digbys what had upset you?"

"They were both out, but I told Nicholas. I was feeling frantic. I *had* to tell somebody, and he was so kind and dear."

"How did he take your—your revelation?"

"Well, not lightly exactly, because he could see the state I was in, but he said he was convinced there was no danger to me. He even thought you might have been misinformed or had put a wrong construction on—on my father's death."

"That was natural and humane. No doubt he tried to calm you."

"No, he really meant it. He asked me to marry him."

"Asked you to *marry* him—immediately after he had been told such a story?"

"He did indeed. He said I was as sane as could possibly be, and that I should remain sane. He pointed out that you really knew nothing but the bald facts about my father, that he could have been ill and in a delirium when he threw himself overboard, and that the moods which frightened you so much were explained by his fear that he would share his mother's fate. As Nicholas says, and after all he *is* a doctor, if she was mad, poor thing, it could have been brought about by a variety of reasons—illness, or an accident. To hear him say such things and to realize their truth—it meant—it meant— oh, I can't describe how much it meant. I was so gloriously happy, and I knew then how much I cared for him. Nicholas said that you must be the first to hear of our engagement, that although, if I wished, we could keep it quiet for a little while, it must not be a secret from you. He made me promise to tell you at once."

"That was courteous and considerate of him," Ursula said, speaking slowly and thoughtfully.

"He put such an emphasis on it." Arabel laughed as

she spoke, her heart uplifted. "He said I was to be sure to tell you that I was no longer in the least bit worried, but that I felt happy and safe and was very, very glad to know I belonged to him."

"I see."

"The relief of having told him is almost as great as the happiness. Nicholas knows everything about me—about the dreams and sleepwalking and feeling so dazed and stupid half the time. I told him that although you put such faith in the tisanes, I was sure they didn't agree with me, as I had felt quite different lately."

"No, they couldn't have agreed with you." Ursula's voice was expressionless, but it was as though each word was dragged from her. "But are you sure, Arabel? I know you like Nicholas Digby—but marriage is so important—the most important thing that can happen to a girl."

"I'm absolutely sure." Arabel's smile was radiant.

"And I suppose you expect me to give my consent to your marriage? Without it you will have to wait for over a year, until you come of age."

"Nicholas won't want to wait as long as that, Ursula. There's no reason why we should, and certainly no reason why you should refuse your consent."

"I am not so certain of that, my dear. I'm compelled to remind you that you are a rich woman, and I hardly think Nicholas Digby has an income to match yours. Moreover he has been seriously ill, during which time many of his patients must have drifted away from him."

"If so, they will soon drift back to him. Dear Ursula, money really isn't as important as you seem to think, and I am so terribly happy—at peace as I never thought I could be after hearing such—such awful things. Now, won't you please wish me joy?"

"Dear child, what mother would not wish it?"

"Then . . ." Arabel raised the glass of champagne to her lips.

On the same instant Mrs. Gibson stretched out her

hand for her own glass, moving so roughly, so clumsily, that the small table between them tipped in Arabel's direction and fell against her. The result, as might have been expected, was that the champagne in Arabel's glass spilled over, drenching her light silk dress. She dropped the almost empty glass and uttered a dismayed exclamation that her mother echoed.

"Oh Arabel, what a pity. Your pretty dress—one of my favorites! Wait, while I get a towel from the bathroom, and let us hope it won't leave a stain."

Picking up the fallen glass she hastened from the room, and it was only a matter of seconds before the glass was thoroughly rinsed. No vestige remained of the sediment that had been at the bottom of it. She returned to her room still holding it and with a towel draped over her arm.

Both of them rubbed at the spreading stain on the bodice and skirt of the silk gown, and Mrs. Gibson said, "That unsteady table! So stupid of me. I should have remembered. But there's plenty of champagne left. I'll pour you out another glass."

Arabel shook her head, "No—please don't. I'd rather not have it. Somehow—I don't know, the moment . . . the right moment has passed. But I'm so glad I've told you, Ursula."

"So am I." Although Ursula's gladness had its roots in reasons that Arabel did not remotely suspect, it was sincere.

Arabel kissed her mother, whose arms went round her. She said,

"I hope you don't think I was too severe with Charlotte, but to creep to your room each night has started up quite a lot of talk. You know what servants are . . . Bessie said she did wonder if Charlotte had seen Lady Thora's ghost, and if that was why she was afraid to sleep there."

"What a horrible idea!" Tears rose in Arabel's eyes.

"A ghost! Why should anyone think . . . ? She is at rest, poor darling."

"These ignorant girls," said Mrs. Gibson, "are always superstitious and have such morbid notions. Naturally I spoke severely to Bessie."

"It's two or three nights since Charlotte slept with me. It wasn't really so odd that she was lonely; she's been accustomed to sleeping in a school dormitory with other girls."

"And that's where she should be now—at school. She hasn't fitted in particularly well with us, and for some unaccountable reason she is hostile to me. However—it is too late to go into all that now. It has been a most distressing day and I feel worn out."

And she looked it, thought Arabel with concern, with her gray pallor and her breathing that had become curiously labored. "It's my turn now to look after you," Arabel said. "A hot drink and bed, Ursula, and tomorrow everything will seem quite different."

Tomorrow it did. Nicholas drove over during the morning and Mrs. Gibson greeted him courteously. She still looked far from well and admitted to a headache, caused, she insisted, by a restless night. Somewhat to Arabel's relief, she and Ursula were alone by the time Nicholas arrived. Cosette Wentworth, an even earlier visitor than Nicholas, had driven up in her new, smart carriage, a victoria, of which she was proud, and had taken Charlotte off with her to do some shopping. Kit, announcing that he had come to a difficult patch in his book, had set off for a walk. The exercise and the fresh air might clear his confused thoughts, or so he hoped. They were not to wait luncheon for him, as he would probably have some bread and cheese and beer at one of the country inns he passed on his way.

Mrs. Gibson, Nicholas, and Arabel forgathered in the

library, and nothing could have been more natural than the older woman's concern for her daughter.

"I want my child to be happy, as any mother would," she said. "She tells me that she has confided in you all I was obliged to reveal. Marriage should never be entered lightly; hazards there must always be, but in this case they are manifold. You are not only several years older than Arabel but also a doctor, and therefore you probably know better than I exactly what risks you are facing. I had previously feared that marriage was impossible for Arabel, and that was one reason why the teaching profession seemed so suitable for her." A wintry smile flashed, as Mrs. Gibson added, "Few schoolmistresses marry—either because they are not drawn to it, or because they have little opportunity to meet members of the opposite sex. It would not have been unusual had Arabel remained single. But now her circumstances are altered. Rich and beautiful as she is, I can see the hardship of it, but one has to consider the danger. . . ."

"You have exaggerated it, I think," said Nicholas quietly, and went on to expound his point of view, saying much that he had already said to Arabel.

Mrs. Gibson listened attentively, seeming ready enough to be convinced, for she occasionally murmured an assenting word. Watching her narrowly, Nicholas realized that his doubts and suspicions were rapidly evaporating. In his mind he had done this kindly woman a vile injustice; nothing could be more motherly than her attitude to Arabel. She smiled at her tenderly from time to time, as she sat beside Nicholas with her hand clasped in his.

"If you are absolutely convinced of the rightness of this marriage, I will not refuse my consent," she said, "which in any case would be operative for only a year or so. Your arguments are plausible, and they have evidently convinced Arabel. I love her too well to allow my own doubts to stand in the way of her happiness, and I make only one stipulation, Nicholas. Give yourself a few weeks—give Arabel a few weeks—before you announce your engagement. If during that time either of you wish to withdraw, there should be no reproaches from you or from her. Will you agree to this?"

"It is for Arabel to say," Nicholas replied.

"And what *do* you say, my dear?" Ursula asked.

Arabel did not hesitate. "I think it's reasonable . . . only fair to Nicholas. The risk is all on his side. If he should change his mind . . ."

"My darling girl, you know I shall do nothing of the kind, though your mother's stipulation, as you say, is not unreasonable. This doesn't mean that we shall see less of each other, or that we cannot make our plans for the future . . . a wedding in the early spring, I hope, if that is not too soon for you, my love."

"Next month would not be too soon for me. Does that seem disgracefully bold, unmaidenly? I know girls are supposed to demur, to prefer a long engagement, but it must be a pretence . . . I mean, if you truly care for a—a lover, isn't it natural to want to belong to him?"

"Beautifully natural," said Nicholas.

"Well, that's how I feel, though my mother is right, I expect. Would six weeks be long enough?"

"Too long, though just about bearable."

Arabel moved nearer to him, and he put his arm round her. Regardless of her mother's presence, he kissed her.

"We must hope for the best," said Mrs. Gibson, forcing a cheerful note into her voice and smiling at them.

The cheerfulness, at least, was not altogether forced, for if Nicholas had had any doubt of her, any fugitive suspicion, she was convinced that this was now allayed. And perhaps she had been altogether wrong in fancying that a warning had been conveyed, though it had seemed clear enough when Arabel had said that Nicholas insisted she must be the first to hear of his proposal, and had emphasized that she was now in his care, happy and protected. It was probable, Mrs. Gibson now reassured herself, that she had misinterpreted the significance of that message.

At least there was now a breathing space, and she was by no means at the end of her resources. Much could happen in six weeks.

# CHAPTER 12

Charlotte was not told there was a secret understanding between Nicholas and Arabel, but she suspected it. Her friend's reticence did not hurt her feelings, for she was at an age when secrets between two people who loved each other seemed deeply romantic. She adored Arabel and was fond of Nicholas; it would be lovely if they married. Nicholas would be good to Arabel, she mused; he wasn't selfish or domineering. Through him she would realize many of her dreams, and they were beautifully unselfish dreams.

Perhaps, thought Charlotte hopefully, they would let her stay with them sometimes when they were married. The conviction that an engagement was pending partly assuaged her disappointment and resentment over the early termination of her stay at Troy Court. Nevertheless it was an effort to be civil to Mrs. Gibson, though the arrangement agreed upon must have come to an end when Arabel married. Charlotte guessed that this would be in the early spring, for there was no reason why the engagement should be a long one.

Who would then live at Troy Court? Mrs. Gibson, probably—at least for a time. Charlotte vaguely supposed that it was legally her home until Arabel came of age, and Nicholas wouldn't want to live there with a mother-in-law who "hovered." He had a house in London that had been unoccupied during his long illness. It was a pleasant old house in Hampstead with a walled garden. Arabel would be sure to like it, and because of Nicholas's Harley Street practice it would be necessary for them to live in London except for holidays and weekends.

This passing reflection reminded Charlotte that her own work, the historical essay she was supposed to be writing, was lagging, though she was writing it at Kit's suggestion, and at the start had been enthusiastic, resolved that it should impress him by its brilliance. But so many upsetting things had occurred within the last few days, and she sensed that Kit was no longer particularly interested. He was always friendly but he looked sad and preoccupied. Perhaps it was due to stress over the book he was writing. It must be terrible for a writer when a book, which had started well, suddenly lost it reality. Was that what had happened to Kit's?

Soon he would be leaving Troy Court for Bloomsbury, and perhaps he might find it easier to work there. His mother's possessiveness must irk him, and, beautiful though Troy Court was, he might be conscious, as Charlotte was uneasily conscious, of a cloud that seemed to hang over it.

Without Kit it would be almost dismal, thought Charlotte. She would miss him terribly, though they would always be friends, she resolved. Her mother would be sympathetic, and when she came out the following year and parties were given for her, she would see to it that Kit was invited to them. He wouldn't refuse such invitations, she was sure of it.

Would he be best man at Arabel's wedding? Would she be chief bridesmaid? It seemed likely, and thinking of herself and Kit in this promising juxtaposition, she was cheered and decided that she really would put in two hours of solid work.

This had been her excuse for absenting herself after dinner. Arabel had said that she must not work later than ten o'clock, and to this Charlotte had agreed. Arabel would be sure to look in on her, for she had said that by then she, as well as Charlotte, would be ready for bed.

While thus musing, she had been digging the fine, long point of her pencil into the sheet of paper before her, and now, to her annoyance, it broke off. As she had worn down the points of other pencils in the desk, she would have to search for a penknife. The little desk had been well stocked for her, and she had seen one either in a drawer or a pigeonhole.

Charlotte was naturally untidy and had often been rebuked for this while at Seacrest College. Papers littered the desk, and sheets of her half-written essay had fallen to the floor. She rose to stack them together, and while she did so there was a gentle knock on the door. As she turned toward it, it opened and Ursula came in.

"Don't let me disturb you," she said genially. "I am off to bed early. I don't suppose I shall sleep, but Arabel has kindly offered to read to me for a while. It has turned so chilly; I wondered if you had a good fire. Have you a full scuttle of coal . . . and in your bedroom too? The maids sometimes tend to be forgetful, but the one on duty has orders to bank up the fires during the evening."

Surprised by this visitation, which was unprecedented, Charlotte assured Mrs. Gibson that she had never been neglected, and the other seemed satisfied. "We must," she said, "look after you well while you are here, but old houses are draughty. I had better peep into the Chinese room to be certain it is warm and comfortable. Arabel catches cold so easily."

One cold, though Charlotte, and that months ago! How the woman did fuss, and of late she often looked really peculiar . . . placid and healthy one minute, and then the next quite ill. What *was* it in that comely face that sometimes produced such a disagreeable effect? Its expression was kindly, there were constant smiles, but those smiles were rarely reflected in the eyes.

I really detest her, thought the girl, and was slightly appalled, for she couldn't remember that she had ever before detested anyone, and this, after all, was the beloved Arabel's mother.

"Good night, then, my dear." Another smile flashed. A subdued Charlotte returned the salutation.

The door closed on Mrs. Gibson, and for a full minute Charlotte was deep in thought. The visit had disturbed her far more than seemed justified. She knew well that Ursula would be the last to care whether or not she was warm and comfortable, but even so it wasn't extraordinary that she had looked in out of curiosity. She must have seen the light shining beneath the door.

"Perhaps," reflected Charlotte, "she thought I was in bed and asleep and had forgotten to blow out the candles. In that case I suppose it would have been natural for her to come in to find out."

She sighed and realized that it was as well she was soon leaving Troy Court. Officially Mrs. Gibson was as much her hostess as Arabel, and how could she stay here, now that this shuddering aversion had taken possession of her?

Still abstracted, Charlotte picked up her papers, glanced through them, put them together, and started on her search for a penknife. She turned out the contents of the little drawers with impatient hands, pushing her fingers into the pigeonholes, for these were unusually deep for such a toy of a desk.

Suddenly she was startled, alert. Sensitive finger-tips had touched a small, round protrusion, which being rough appeared to be of a different wood. It moved in obedience to pressure, spun round with the velocity of a top, and then before Charlotte's startled gaze the left side of the desk slid smoothly back, and she saw a compartment beyond the pigeonhole. Few things being more excitingly delightful than to discover a secret room, passage or drawer—in precisely this order of excitement—Charlotte's eyes glowed. Had anyone else made this discovery? She doubted it. If Arabel had been aware of the secret drawer she would have told her. Was it empty?

It was not. Fingers probing farther discovered a book, a soft binding, thin leaves, a square of cardboard tucked away between them. Almost reluctantly, because to find so much through touch was thrilling, Charlotte drew forth the prize. The book was not large, but it was thick and of more than pocketbook size. The cover was of limp brown leather, across which in tarnished gilt was written the word "Diary." She riffled through the leaves, which were closely covered with a delicate Italianate writing. This on the first page was more flamboyant. Capital letters were scrolled with a flourish, "My Journal," and beneath was the name "Thora" and the date of the year. Twenty-one years ago, thought Charlotte awestruck.

It was strange indeed, even eerie, to be reading what a dead woman had written so many years ago, but Charlotte's curiosity could not be restrained. Every page in the book had been used, and Lady Thora had meticulously dated each entry. Glancing at the last page Charlotte saw that the journal had come to an end nearly four years ago.

Today we returned to Troy Court. It is Arabel's birthday, and, for the first time in years, I am free from anxiety about her. In London I was successful and managed to evade Ursula. While she shopped, I saw the solicitor I had written to from Italy He had followed out my instructions and had prepared the draft of my will, which I signed in his office and which was duly witnessed. Arabel's future is safe.

Charlotte remembered then that it was in this small, elegant desk, which seemed so much of a toy that one would scarcely expect it to hold anything of importance, that Lady Thora's will had been discovered, almost by accident. She read on avidly,

I have deceived Ursula, mostly by hints and half-promises, for she will expect more than I have bequeathed to her, but through the years I have given her so much more than her salary, and this has been used for the benefit of her son. Troy Court belongs to Arabel, which is hers by right, and indeed all I possess. If this brings about the scandal that during my lifetime I have made so many heartbreaking sacrifices to avoid, it cannot be helped. There is no room in this book to write any more.

The latter statement was true enough, for the last words had been written on the inside of the cover. As Charlotte turned to the beginning of the book, the square of cardboard her fingers had touched while her trophy was yet hidden from her, dropped to the floor. She stooped to pick it up and gazed at a small photograph, once glossy but now slightly yellow with age. Photographs, with the subject stiffly posed, were often lifelessly wooden, but this photograph was an exception. A young man, clean-shaven save for sideburns, and with a thatch of curly, black hair, stood behind a carved chair, with arms folded on the back of it. The photographer had contrived to catch the personality—dancing liveliness in fine, dark eyes, a confident smile on up-curved lips, an impudent tilt to the head poised on broad shoulders. It was a handsome face, so handsome indeed that it could have been called beautiful. Of whom did it hauntingly remind her? There was a faint resemblance to Lord Byron in his youth, but a much more insistent likeness to a face familiar to Charlotte. A second later it flashed upon her. The original of the portrait could have been Arabel's brother, her twin brother, resembling her as Kit certainly did not. On the back of the portrait one word was written, not in Lady Thora's delicate handwriting but in a heavy masculine scrawl, "BENITO."

A second interruption, a knock on the door! Charlotte instinctively drew her blotting pad over the journal. But when Arabel came in, she did not glance at the desk, taking it for granted that Charlotte was working.

She had promised to look in at ten o'clock and had kept her word. Having duly read aloud to Mrs. Gibson until the latter was drowsy, she was now off to bed and told Charlotte that it was time she did the same. Charlotte, dazed, assured her that she would. Arabel lightly kissed her cheek, said good-night, and left her.

As the door again closed, Charlotte, without any consideration that Lady Thora's journal, though found by her, was Arabel's property, once more plunged into a bout of absorbing reading.

Charlotte's heart was now thudding with excitement. She was tingling with a half-forced suspicion, aware that she had stumbled on a story well hidden for many years. Rapidly she skimmed through the first pages of the journal, which for the main part chronicled social events—a dance given by a Lady Lucian.

I wore pink gauze trimmed with silver roses. Cousin Georgina chaperoned me, but she spent most of the evening in the cardroom, and Captain Atholl persuaded me to grant him too many dances. Some of the dowagers looked at me disapprovingly, especially as there were several girls who were wallflowers, poor things. I tried to commend them to the attentions of my partners, but gentlemen are not kind enough to sacrifice themselves to plain girls who dance badly. Captain Atholl said I was the undoubted belle, and that in Georgian days I should have been a toast. I was flattered, but oh, how I wished B. could have been there—a social equal—or that young Lochinvar he could have carried me away on Ranger, looking like a prince on that fine horse. Not that there is any question of an unwanted husband for me—at least not yet, though Cousin Georgina hints it is time I should be thinking of marriage. What a horrible notion, feeling as I do about my wonderful B.

The "wonderful B.," she discovered, was an Italian riding master, engaged by Lord Riba to give his daughter lessons. Two or three times a week he rode over from Storkley on Ranger, his splendid black horse with a white star on his forehead. Lady Thora gleefully related that there was nobody to chaperon her on these occasions, as her Cousin Georgina did not ride; nor did her father, who was subject to the gout but was anxious that his daughter should acquit herself well on horseback. Lady Thora confessed she had a poor seat and would have detested the exercise but for B. She was not supposed during these lessons to ride beyond the grounds, and rarely did, but there came the day when the horses were tethered and they strolled in the home wood, which was as solitary as though they were miles away from Troy Court. Lady Thora and B. were by now in love and in despair about it, for how could they ever marry? B. had come to England to help his aunt's husband with his livery stables. The aunt was an Italian woman who had married an Englishman. B. would not stay at Storkley for more than a few months. But they could not be parted, wrote Lady Thora distractedly; they would elope, and although her father would be very angry, he would eventually forgive them.

The last words were edged in at the bottom of the page and, about to turn the page in order to continue, Charlotte involuntarily raised her head. By now everyone in the house must have retired, yet she was sure that she had heard stealthy footsteps. Scarcely audible though these were, they had penetrated through her intense concentration, but in the fascination of reading the journal had been impatiently ignored.

Now, though still vividly fascinated, the past for an instant receded, and she was conscious of her isolation in Lady Thora's suite at the end of the corridor. Complete silence would have been natural, but to her strained fancy it had not been absolute—a board had creaked, there had been a faint rustling, the sense of a near presence . . .

Charlotte shivered. How easy it would be to imagine that she was *not* alone, that the ghost of the romantic girl who had written this journal so many years ago had briefly returned to look over her shoulder as she read it. A strangely urgent impression, but Charlotte's native common sense conquered it. What if a board had creaked? That wasn't unusual in an old house . . . as for the slight rustling, there were draughts, as Mrs. Gibson had said, to stir rugs and window curtains.

She wished she could put that smiling face out of her mind. Falsely smiling! Falsely benevolent, for, from time to time, the woman was unable to conceal her dislike. Her own presence here, thought Charlotte, was more than a mild inconvenience. Mrs. Gibson actively resented it and not solely through jealously. That, if she really loved Arabel, could be forgiven; it wouldn't have been unnatural. Charlotte's mother had once said that jealousy was one of the drawbacks of maternity and had to be fought if one was not to hamper a young life.

But Mrs. Gibson didn't love Arabel. Suddenly, Charlotte, who had always doubted, was convinced of it. She fussed to an extraordinary degree, but that was different. One had only to contrast her expression when her eyes rested on Kit to know that he alone was in possession of her heart. How ghastly, how inexpressibly awful it would be for the girl who married Kit. Her one chance would be for them to live at the other end of the world.

With determination, Charlotte dismissed the thought. Everything was quiet now, genuinely quiet. She turned the flimsy page of the diary and read on,

I think I should go out of my mind but for Ursula. She is so dear and understanding and will take messages. There is nobody else in whom I can confide.

Soon the entries in the journal were tragic ones. The illicit love was discovered, and Lord Riba was wrathful and blamed Cousin Georgina, the middle-aged duenna. She left for her home in Ireland in high dudgeon. B. and Lady Thora were parted. After a stormy scene he left the neighborhood never to return; so did his relations. Money could accomplish anything, lamented Lady Thora. It had cost Papa a fortune to ship them all to Australia. B. said he had no choice but to submit. The livery stable was not paying; he had no money, and Lady Thora had nothing but her allowance. If there was talk, it was evident that it had been hushed up, and nobody suspected that Ursula Gibson had helped the lovers. Lady Thora vowed that all happiness was over for her. Worse was to come when Lord Riba died suddenly of a heart attack, and Lady Thora blamed herself for the shock and worry, which she was sure had caused it. Then came a startling entry,

I scarcely know how to write it, even in my own private journal that nobody will ever see as it is hidden in the secret compartment of my desk. Even dear Ursula does not know that this exists. My love for B. is fated to have a RESULT. What shall I do—what can I do? I have no idea of his address in Australia. I cannot write to him, begging him to return. Besides . . . would I marry him now, even if I could? I do not think so, for I cannot forget that at Papa's bidding he signed a paper vowing he would never again set foot in England or communicate with me. He gave me up for money, whereas had he been a true knight as I thought once, he would have refused and carried me off in secret. I can thank God that dear Papa died without suspecting the wrong I did. Ursula says she can and will help me. She has a PLAN. Poor Ursula is in grief herself, for her husband, who has died while at sea, though from what she has told me about him, this may be a blessing in disguise. We must go abroad, she says, and nobody need ever know, for it will be thought that the child is hers, born posthumously. She will adopt it, and then I need not be parted from my little one.

Although Charlotte had half-suspected this denouement, she gasped. So that was it! Oh, poor Lady Thora! But it explained all, and what a cunning, hateful role Ursula Gibson had played. Had she ever really loved the hapless Lady Thora? Charlotte doubted it, but she had used her, and by threats veiled as persuasion, she had at last completely dominated her. Arabel, the child upon whom Lady Thora lavished a passionate, secret love, had been allowed to stay at Troy Court for only a few years. Ill health and the fear of scandal had kept Lady Thora in subjection, and of course Ursula Gibson had cared nothing at all for the child who was ostentibly her daughter. The later entries in the journal revealed only too plainly that Lady Thora had had little say in Arabel's upbringing and had been too ill to put up much of a fight for her. It had been Ursula who had insisted on foreign travel, saying that sojourns abroad might cure her employer's crippling rheumatism. She had dragged the exhausted woman hither and thither and had made her promise that, on her death, all she possessed would be left to her housekeeper. Yet in the end Lady Thora had outwitted her. Poor thing, how desperate she must have been when she had secretly given instructions to an unknown London lawyer.

After Lady Thora's death, Mrs. Gibson had no doubt hunted for a later will than that in the local solicitor's care, for she had been repeatedly told there was one. She must have supposed it was safely lodged with Mr. Brecknell, until he denied all knowledge of it. The relief and triumph of finding the later will had been of short duration, and her anger when she discovered its contents profound.

"I know now that I was right. Ever since then, she has been trying to bring about Arabel's death, as though by accident." Charlotte was so carried away that she spoke the words aloud, and then shot a scared glance around for fear that even in her own sitting room she had been overheard.

Now, for the first time, it struck her that she was in possession of information that Arabel might wish to keep to herself, but hard on this came the reflection that if she did, it would be the worst thing possible. The sense of guilt was exorcised, for the only sensible thing, the only safe course, was for the truth to be generally known. Then the hateful Mrs. Gibson would be rendered harmless. Arabel might be foolish enough to think the story could be kept within the family, but that simply would not do. When Kit and Charlotte both left Troy Court, who could tell what "accident" might befall her? She would then be at the mercy of the woman whom the world believed to be her devoted mother.

Poor, poor Kit to have such a mother. But mercifully he wasn't in the least like her in disposition. The Herald family, who had seemed to treat her so harshly, had been justified in their dislike of her.

Charlotte glanced at the clock and saw with amazement that it was past one o'clock, and here she was, still dressed, and with not the least tendency to sleep. The journal was now an embarrassment to her, and she was eager to hand it over to Arabel, but it was too late—or rather, too early. Arabel must be asleep by now, and the journal must be hidden until Charlotte could get her alone. She would have restored it to the secret compartment of the desk, except that she could not discover how to close it. The empty space gaped at her. The rough round knob that manipulated the panel had disappeared when that part of the desk slid aside.

Charlotte finally decided that the book would be safe

under her pillow, and she put it there and then started to get undressed. The fire had burnt low, and the candles in both rooms were guttering. Feverish with excitement that she was sure would keep her awake for hours, she could not endure the prospect of being left in the dark, and she remembered that candles on brackets were placed at intervals along the corridor and invariably snuffed by either Mrs. Gibson or Arabel when they retired. One of these she would appropriate while her candle was still flickering, for in the darkness it might be impossible to find the brackets.

But it was not dark outside! This was the first thing to impinge upon Charlotte's senses. Far down the corridor there was a hot, red light that leaped and danced upon the walls, the floor, the ceiling. It came from the open door of the Chinese room. Charlotte stared at it terrified, for now there was the acrid sent of burning fabric and a curl of smoke eddying down the corridor toward her. She screamed and hurled herself forward, tripping over a rug and leaving behind her the bedroom slippers which were comfortably large and which she called "shufflers." As she ran, she screamed again and again, hoping to be heard, though realizing that the servants all slept behind the baize door at the far end of the wing, and that the baize door muffled sound.

She reached the threshold of the Chinese room, and for a moment the scene was so fantastic that she stood spellbound. The silk panels were alight, and as the door and window were both open, the figures on them shook and quivered as though they had been brought to life, with the red flames illuminating them.

Arabel was still asleep. Charlotte could see her dark head on the pillow of the big bed. A chair between the walls and the bed had already caught fire, and Charlotte literally leaped over the threshold, conscious of, but not identifying, a bulky obstruction that lay in her path. She shook Arabel violently by the shoulder and pulled her out of the bed.

"What—what is it?" Arabel muttered drowsily.

"Fire! The room is on fire. Hurry!" Acting instinctively she pulled a quilt off the bed and wrapped it around Arabel. Oh, why wouldn't she do something to help herself, she thought despairingly. But Arabel stood like a statue, ignoring the spreading flames and staring with horror at the motionless form that lay between the fireplace and the door.

Then, thrusting Charlotte aside, she was kneeling beside it, touching hand and cheek, her voice broken and entreating. When she looked up at last, it was to say, "She's dead, I'm afraid, but we can't leave her here. You must help me, Charlotte."

Between them they dragged the inert body into the corridor and to Charlotte's supreme relief were joined by Kit. He bent over his mother briefly, and then sent Charlotte skittering along the polished floor to wake the servants.

Meanwhile, he was dragging down bed hangings and curtains and piling rugs against the walls in an effort to smother the flames. Soon the servants were on the scene and Kit was helped by the butler and footman. Buckets were filled with water and passed from hand to hand, and the bootboy was sent to rouse the coachman and grooms in their quarters above the stables.

By the time one of these had saddled a horse to ride into Storkley and give the alarm to the fire brigade, the fire was under control. It had not spread beyond the Chinese room, though that was irretrievably ruined. Most of the furniture was badly scorched, the floor and ceiling blackened, and the silk paneling hung in flaking rags.

Two of the manservants had lifted Ursula Gibson's body and carried it to her room. Kit and Arabel gazed at each other with sorrow and shocked bewilderment. "The fire didn't touch her," said Kit, in a shaking voice of grief. "She must have died of fright."

Within hours this mystery at least was elucidated. Ursula Gibson's death had been caused by a heart attack. She could not, Dr. Galbraith told Kit and Arabel, have been in ignorance of her condition, for there were tablets in her medicine cupboard that had been prescribed by a well-known London doctor, who at the inquest was to testify that he had recently been consulted by the dead woman.

Although Charlotte was eager to be rid of the journal, it was not immediately possible to hand it over to Arabel, grieving for her supposed mother's death. There were limits, Charlotte argued, to what anyone could be expected to bear.

Within the next twenty-four hours it became plain to her that the "understanding" between Nicholas and Arabel that she had suspected was indeed a fact, for in her grief Arabel openly turned to him for comfort, and as the Digby's insisted that at this time it would be better for Charlotte to be at Green Lawns, she had the opportunity to speak to him alone, and with great relief to hand the journal over to him, begging him to give it to Arabel.

"I dare say it was wrong of me to read all that Lady Thora wrote in it," Charlotte admitted, when she had described the finding of the journal, "but at the time I was so excited, so enthralled, that that truly didn't strike me, and whether right or wrong it's just as well I did read it, for now you can break it to her that that horrible woman wasn't her mother. It's a hundred times better to be illegitimate. Or don't you think so? But you must, Nick, for she was a murderess in intention. Arabel doesn't suspect it, and I don't suppose she ever will, not even when she reads Lady Thora's journal, but although the cause of the fire is a mystery to everyone, it isn't . . . what I mean is, it's no mystery to me. Mrs. Gibson started it—she planned it. . . ."

"Charlotte, there's no proof of that." Nicholas had listened in almost complete silence, but now he checked her with authority. "We have only the flimsiest suspicions, which few would take seriously, that Arabel's adopted mother even wished, let alone attempted, to harm her. . . ."

"Those suspicions are certainties to me, Nick. That evening Mrs. Gibson came to my room when I was working, a thing she never did in the ordinary way, with some utterly unnecessary talk about fires being built up and hoping the maids had seen to it, and so on. She said she intended to see the Chinese room was properly warm for Arabel. Oh, it all amounted to nothing, but she intended it to be remembered afterwards if . . . if Arabel perished; her concern for Arabel, her complaint that the maids were careless and neglectful. There were wire guards to put up before the bedroom and sitting room fires, and Arabel and I have always been careful about that; but in all the confusion of that dreadful night I saw that the fireguard in the Chinese room was lying on the ground near to where Mrs. Gibson was lying. And within reach of her hand—one arm was flung out—there was a wax taper. It was still alight and had fallen on a fur rug which was smouldering. I put my foot on it, not then realizing the significance, but I realize it now. She had set light to the silk wall panels with that taper, Nick, though people have said since that the fire must have started through a coal falling from the grate. But there *were* no fallen coals. She might have raked some out as a finishing touch . . . I don't know . . . she hadn't time for finishing touches, for her heart gave out and she collapsed, which was an easier death than she deserved, the wicked woman."

"Have you spoken about this to anyone else?" Nicholas asked.

"No—only to you." Charlotte burst into sobs, and through sobs, uttered, "I couldn't keep it to myself any longer . . . it was too much . . . I've been feeling frantic inside."

"Yes, yes, of course you have." Nicholas put his arm round her comfortingly.

"I shall never tell anyone else; I don't want anyone else to know. She's dead and can do no further harm, and it's Kit I think of now. She *was* his mother, and it would be terrible for him to know how wicked she was. I won't have him hurt any more."

"This is something we must both try to forget," Nicholas said, though it struck him that when Kit heard the true facts of Arabel's birth, he would have his own doubts about his mother. What could explain her insistence that Arabel was mentally unstable, and that this was inherited through Bernard Gibson, who might or might not have been insane, but who was certainly not her father? Nicholas's pity for Kit was profound, and it did not occur to him then, though it did later, that Charlotte was more than ordinarily concerned for Kit.


Nicholas, with a brief explanation, gave Arabel the journal that was to explain so much to her, and, when doing so, begged her not to read it until after the funeral.

"If you look at the desk in Charlotte's sitting room, you will see for yourself how she chanced to find the journal," he said. "No doubt there's a way of closing the panel again, but she couldn't discover it."

Arabel gazed wonderingly at the book, glanced at the first page, but then closed it. "I won't read it yet," she promised. "Have you?"

"No—though Charlotte did, which strictly speaking she had no right to do. But it was understandable in her excitement at finding it. She told me the gist of the story that Lady Thora told. . . ."

"An important story, Nicholas?"

"Yes, darling, it is, though nothing is really important except that you and I have found each other and love each other. The present and the future belong to us. Isn't that what really matters?"

"It's natural we should think so," Arabel agreed. "Lovers are terribly egotistical, aren't they?"

"They have to be."

"Though just now Ursula is the first thought in Kit's mind and in mine too. It would be heartless if she was not. Kit thinks she must have awakened and smelled something burning and that she realized it was coming from the Chinese room and tried to save me but collapsed. It's a comforting thought to him, Nicholas."

And a completely erroneous one, Nicholas silently reflected.

Arabel said, "I don't forget it was Charlotte who actually saved my life. It was wonderfully brave of her, but Ursula was also brave. That doctor in London pronounced her doom, but she was determined Kit and I should not know. She carried on as usual, intending to spare us as long as she could. I dare say she thought that as she had been forced to tell me about my father, I had enough to bear."

Nicholas also thought that at the present time Arabel had enough to bear. He could not be sure how she would take the truth as revealed by Lady Thora's journal, but her opinion of Ursula Gibson was bound to suffer a drastic change.

As it happened, Arabel did not glance at the journal again until the following week. After the funeral, there was a reading of Ursula Gibson's will, a simple document in which she left all she possessed to Kit, which was just as it should be, Arabel said, showing no sign that she was hurt because Ursula had not even mentioned her name. It was as though she had had no daughter, only a son. It was a heart-searing day, but Arabel was a little comforted when Cosette Wentworth drove over and insisted that both Kit and Arabel return with her to the Tower House for a few days.

"Your housekeeper will see that the place is put in

order before you return," said Cosette, brisk and kindly. "You can close up the Chinese room, can't you? You will have to have the workmen in later on. There are always such sad things to do after a death, but there is no reason why you shouldn't delay for a little while." And then Cosette added, evidently with a full appreciation of the situation, "The Tower House is no farther from Green Lawns, and Nicholas and Charlotte can drive over every day. Kit, why don't you bring your manuscript and such books as you need with you? A room can be fixed up for you to work in without interruption, if you are inclined to work."

Kit thanked her and followed the suggestion, aware that work on a book that took him far back into the past would mean hours of forgetfulness. He had already thought too long and too painfully of his mother, of her many sacrifices for him, and of the short while they had had together.

Thus it was that Lady Thora's journal that Arabel had locked in a bureau drawer was left there and forgotten. But when she returned a week later, she remembered it.

She was now occupying Lady Thora's suite, for Charlotte was still at Green Acres, and it seemed fitting that she should read her life story in the room where she had spent so much of her time. Opening the journal, it now seemed strange to Arabel that she had felt so little curiosity, for Nicholas had told her it was an important story, although having said this he had said no more, and Charlotte, who was very subdued these days, and who, on visiting at the Tower House, had spent most of her time with Kit, had not alluded to her find.

Lately, Arabel had found it difficult to fix her attention on anything for long, and she had not expected to read more than a few pages at a sitting. Nor might she have done for the first entries were trivial and not particularly interesting, but then, glancing through the pages, she came upon the photograph, which Charlotte had slipped into an envelope. Instantly, she recognized the likeness to herself. Minutes passed and she was still gazing tranced at that bold, handsome face, but after a while she put it aside and started to read with concentration.

A groom from Troy Court rode over to Green Lawns with a letter for Nicholas, and within half an hour he and Arabel were together. She had waited for him in the library had been pacing the long room, and the book in which Lady Thora had written her love story was still in her hand.

"I had to send for you," Arabel said.

"My darling, of course. I've been expecting it."

"I've only just finished reading all she wrote. I can't understand why I wasn't eager to do so. I suppose I didn't really take it in when you said it was important. I wasn't even sufficiently interested to question Charlotte, though I saw her most days while Kit and I were staying with the Wentworths."

"Mrs. Gibson's death was a great shock to you—that and the fire. It blotted out everything else."

"Perhaps it was merciful. I had taken as much as I could for a few days. You said Charlotte told you the gist of what was written here." Arabel put down the book on a nearby table, but her hand still rested on it.

"Yes. How do you feel about it?"

"Thankful—thankful . . . but grieved that I did not know it while she lived. I told you I loved her and try as I would I could never make myself love Ursula, though I deceived myself, insisted that I did. I wonder if this, an inward, instinctive knowledge, was why I could never call her anything but—Ursula. Now it's a—a release to be free of her. It's hard not to think bitterly of her, Nicholas, though I shall try not to. She heartlessly dominated my real mother, and she must have hated me. Why else should she have told me that her second husband, who was supposed to be my father, was mad and his mother before him?"

"That may well have been a—fabrication."

"Yes, there was only her word for it, but she intended me to believe, to fear there was a fatal taint . . . that I was myself unstable and might become a raving lunatic. Why? Did she want me to go mad through suggestion?"

"My dearest, how can anyone tell? I've asked myself . . . she may herself have been unhinged."

"Perhaps her object was to keep me from marrying anyone. She thought I wouldn't dare. She wanted to rule me as she had ruled my mother. Oh Nicholas—to know the truth—the bliss of it. Being born out of wedlock is nothing—or at least not to me."

"It is nothing to me either, my darling. Your mother was a sweet creature, I have no doubt. . . ."

"Oh, she was, she was, and how she must have suffered. Do you suppose I shall ever know anything about my father? He was an Italian and his name was Benito Vidal. But how can one trace a father who went to Australia twenty years ago? He may be dead; he may not even have settled there."

"Do you want to trace him, Arabel?"

"I'm not sure—I haven't had time to think. Probably not. She didn't. Nicholas, must this story be generally known, or can you and I and Charlotte keep it hidden?"

"Is that what you wish?"

"I wish it now—for Kit's sake. He honors his mother's memory. Her possessiveness sometimes irked him, but he thought her noble, self-sacrificing. He could not forgive his father's family because they scorned her. If he should discover that she had done all she could to separate me from my real mother, that not content with this she pretended I was threatened with hereditary madness . . . oh Nicholas, it would be the most dreadful blow to him. Why cannot we leave it as it is—at least for now. Though some day there may be circumstances that will make it necessary for the truth to be told. If so—years hence—well, Kit will be older, established I'm sure as a writer; he will be able to bear it then. But just now, while he is newly bereft and feeling his way, working hard though not with certainty . . . oh, don't you see?"

"Yes, I see. It's a decision that is wise and kind."

"I think of my mother too. Everyone speaks of her as—as perfect. She was horrified of scandal and had long outlived that youthful folly. Can Charlotte keep this secret, do you suppose?"

"I am certain she can." Nicholas was thankful that Arabel did not guess how much more Charlotte was prepared to keep secret. "Charlotte, though young, has a great deal of sense, and this is none of her business."

"Even if it were, I am sure she would prefer Kit not to know. She admires and likes him."

"She is idealistically in love with him"—and Nicholas smiled. "It won't do her any harm. Either she will painlessly outgrow it, or with the years it will become real to them both. Arabel, how soon will you marry me?"

"As soon as you wish—as soon as we can. . . . Is Mr. Brecknell my guardian until I come of age? But even if he is, why should he prevent our marriage or wish to postpone it?"

"I am perfectly sure he won't. My sweet—I want you so much. . . ."

She went into his arms with a smile, "I know . . . I'm so happy to know it, and I shall be so happy too when I am no longer known as Arabel Gibson."

Owing to what was considered a double bereavement, the wedding, planned for a fortnight ahead, was to be a very quiet one. Kit, though he wished Nicholas and Arabel joy, and did indeed hope that she would be happy, was wounded by the speed with which she had forgotten her brief passion for him. He agreed, however, to give her away at the village church ceremony. It would mean little enough, he thought gloomily, as he had already had to give her up. Charlotte begged to be a bridesmaid, and Arabel could not find it in her heart to refuse, though she had intended to dispense with bridesmaids.

Reluctantly, Kit asked, "I take it that Nicholas knows about—well, what Mother told you about your father?"

"Yes, he knows what she told me, but he doesn't attach any importance to it," said Arabel, suppressing the burning indignation that against her will occasionally threatened to overwhelm her.

"Well, as to that, I'm inclined to agree, Bel. I've thought many times that there was nothing much in it. . . . I told you so . . . the effect of the tropics and so on. Mother meant it for the best, but she would have done better not to tell you. Try to forget it."

"I can and I shall," Arabel assured him, her eyes warm with affection as they rested on him. How odd that now, though she knew there was no relationship between them, he really did seem like her brother. "You'll keep in touch, won't you?" she said.

"Of course. We shall both be living in London. You won't often be at Troy Court."

"Not anyway for a few years, but, as you know, I have my plans for the place, and Nicholas approves. Sometimes when we *are* here, Kit, you must stay with us, and I shall ask Charlotte as well. Nicholas and I are so fond of her."

"Then you must continue to meet, if only occasionally."

It might well be, she thought, that Kit would finally find his best and enduring happiness with Charlotte. Time would tell.

## ABOUT THE AUTHOR

LAURA CONWAY is the pseudonym of a well-known English novelist whose stories in the Gothic tradition have delighted thousands of readers in her native country and who is, with this book, making her first appearance in America.

America's Best-Loved Author

# EMILIE LORING

## Now in a Deluxe Boxed Set!

8 enchanting novels of drama and romance by the famous Emilie Loring are now available in a deluxe gift-box set. This beautiful, protective set makes a perfect gift—for someone you love or for yourself.